DAVY BYRNES STORIES 2014

The six prize-winning stories from the
2014 Davy Byrnes Short Story Award
as selected by Anne Enright, Yiyun Li and Jon McGregor

The Stinging Fly

A Stinging Fly Press Book
First published in Dublin in September 2014.

2 4 6 8 9 7 5 3 1

The Stinging Fly Press
PO Box 6016
Dublin 1

www.stingingfly.org

Set in Palatino

Printed by Naas Printing Ltd, County Kildare

978-1-906539-41-2

The Stinging Fly Press gratefully acknowledges the financial support
of The Arts Council / An Chomhairle Ealaíon and Dublin City Council.

Baile Átha Cliath
Dublin City

The 2014 Davy Byrnes Short Story Award was sponsored by Davy Byrnes
and organised by The Stinging Fly with support from
Dublin UNESCO City of Literature.

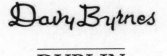

DUBLIN
UNESCO
City of Literature

Contents

2014 Award Winner

Sara Baume   1
Solesearcher1

Short-listed Stories

Trevor Byrne   19
Go Down Sunday

Julian Gough   49
Harvest

Arja Kajermo   75
The Iron Age

Colm McDermott   117
Absence

Danielle McLaughlin   153
The Dinosaurs On Other Planets

Notes on the Authors   181

Acknowledgements   183

Solesearcher1

Sara Baume

2014 Award Winner

Judges' Comments

Beautifully shaped, vividly imagined and realised, this story is the work of an original talent, a writer who has a distinctive vision and the formal discipline the short story requires.

'Solesearcher1' is set in a small town on the Irish coast and the characters in it are creatures of habit. The story shows the moment when that sense of habit becomes strange, difficult and sinister, but there is great pleasure in the writing and this makes a piece that is about loneliness and isolation very enjoyable, somehow, with tenderness and insight on every page.

Author's Note

I used to consider shore angling a somewhat dreary pastime, but I didn't really understand.

The best anglers are able to cast their lead further than the length of two football pitches, and they'd never dream of expending so much line just to catch something for baking in a coat of cheese for supper. The best anglers only care about hooking enormous or uncatchable fish, about dragging up from the blue some creature most of us will live and die without even knowing existed: smooth hound, cuckoo wrasse, tompot blenny, megrim, tope.

The ocean reaches down for almost seven miles at its deepest point, drowns out seventy-one percent of the earth's surface and is believed to contain up to a million different species, at least one third of which have never been identified.

Within Phil's disappointing annexe of the undrowned earth, even the roll of toilet paper in her local pub remains unchanged the whole year through. She goes fishing because this is her only shot at touching the ineffable.

—*Sara Baume*

SHE GOES FISHING EVERY SUNDAY. She sets up two rods every time: one for something she might actually catch, depending upon the weather conditions and the time of year, and one for Dover sole.

A sole is born in the configuration of a regular fish with one eye either side of its body, but as it matures, the left eye migrates to the right and sidles up to its fellow. Now the sole will spend the rest of its life lying down and staring upwards. This is nature's twisted way of allowing an otherwise vulnerable fish to conceal itself within the seabed and keep watch for predators both at once.

Yet the sole is not as susceptible as it looks. Because of its tiny mouth and the mysterious conditions under which it feeds, sole are almost impossible to catch on a line from the shore. In spring, summer and autumn, even experienced anglers under ideal skies using extremely delicate hooks stand only the slightest chance. In winter, there's no chance at all.

Still she puts out a sole line every Sunday, hoping for a miracle.

Phil always expected she'd end up on the dole, but she didn't. Her father, Phil Snr, saw to it that she didn't. Time and time again, he'd tell her it was undignified to stand in the post office queue with an old age pensioner either side and beg scraps from the taxpayer's table. So Phil is a plumber, the only woman plumber she knows. She plumbs because plumbing was her father's trade, and because

! Leabharlanna Fhine Gall

plumbing was her father's trade, nobody in the family ever dared to describe it as 'undignified'.

'I look down people's toilets all day,' Phil tells the weeknight drinkers in the Hope & Anchor.

She goes to the Hope & Anchor every evening after the day's plumbing. Sometimes she talks to the other drinkers, and sometimes she doesn't. She always occupies the same stool and orders a packet of Manhattan Dry Roasted with her first pint and goes out for a smoke after her second and uses the bathroom after her third. The Ladies has never been anything other than deserted, and Phil reckons she must hew away at the same roll of paper for most of each year.

She tends not to think of herself as a woman plumber, nor as a woman, nor as a plumber. She cannot think of herself as a woman because she isn't a mother or a wife; she's only a daughter, and daughters don't count because daughters don't earn or even choose their status. She cannot think of herself as a plumber because she doesn't care about plumbing, and Phil refuses to be defined by the things about which she does not care.

Every weeknight, she goes to her stool in the Hope & Anchor. Every Saturday, she visits her father's house. Every Sunday, she packs her fishing box and drives her plumbing van to the open sea.

Fishing is what Phil cares about. Still seas on overcast days with the box open in her favourite spot and all her hooks and traces and bait tubs in their right place. Phil cares about the grace of the cast. She cares about how fast the line sears the air, how distant the splash of the lead as it breaks the surface. She cares about the way in which the rod tip jerks, about the very particular jerk which proclaims a fish. She cares about precisely and faultlessly reeling back in, but she cares most of all about the exact moment her fish breaches the surface and shows itself.

Bait, cast, jerk, reel, breach: this is what Phil cares about.

Only on Sundays does she cease egging time on until the next thing. Only with saltwater pressing waist-high against her waders does she feel calm, comforted by the squeeze of the sea. Only waiting for a bite is she content to simply wait.

On the first Saturday of the new year, she brings her father bread, milk, meat, tea, onions, carrots and potatoes, but nothing green. Like a fussy child, he's never eaten greens.

Her father lives in a bungalow on a small plot of land bounded on all sides by another man's fodder fields. An unkempt boreen runs from the road into his driveway. Phil Snr has never done anything to make his asphalt and grass seem like a garden. There are only the farmer's electric fences to mark its periphery. Then there's a wheelie bin, a washing line and a concrete coal bunker, nothing else.

The farmer is a compassionless man. He always leaves his cows out in winter and neglects to rotate them from field to field. He never comes to restock their silage troughs at the weekend and so, for two solid days and nights each week, the cows moo hungrily. Phil always remarks on the noise, but her father says it doesn't bother him, that he can't even hear it any more.

After dinner, they sit in the straight-backed armchairs in the good front room and watch television together. Her father always chooses the twenty-four-hour news station. He likes to rest assured that people all over the world are simultaneously suffering a medley of troubles. Phil is always more interested in the weather forecast. Today the weatherwoman wears a jewel bib and bell sleeves as she issues an amber weather warning. The colour-coding of elemental forces irritates Phil. She pictures what an actual amber storm might look like: the trees seeping gemstones, the wind snatching the stones up and spinning them into cyclones of solidified amber. She notices how closely her father watches the weather, and she wonders at the source of such intensity, when he doesn't have anywhere to go any more; when most days, he hardly even sets foot across the bungalow's threshold.

When Phil stands to leave every Saturday evening, Phil Snr always acknowledges her departure by means of the same sentence.

'Be sure and shut the door now,' he always says.

The only fish a person might pull from a stormy sea in winter is cod. So on Sunday Phil casts a cod line into the distance and drops her sole line to the froth not so far beyond her feet. She is cautious as she can be with the wind and waves, still the cod hook is soon snagged by a knot of eelgrass and she can do nothing but tug and tug until the line snaps.

'ASSSSSSHOOOOOOLE!' Phil screams into the wind, addressing the storm.

She isn't angry over the loss of a lead so much as because she's accidentally deposited another small piece of poison in the already much maligned ocean.

There are usually other people on the beach on Sundays, but today there's no one from one end of the strand to the other but Phil. The sand is blanketed by debris either thrown up by the waves or fallen from the cliff tops. The blanketing debris is cut through with rivulets gushing from the fields as hurriedly as though the sea might vanish if they don't reach it in time.

Usually, there are family outings on fine days and walkers even when it's drizzling. There's always at least one loose dog which gallivants up to Phil with its long tongue flapping and tries to snatch a baited hook. On one occasion a husky gulped a ball of crabmeat and ran off with the line trailing up from its belly and flying out between its teeth. The owner came shouting and gesticulating, as angry as if Phil had lured the husky over and sadistically fisted the crab down its throat.

Sometimes she sees people on the beach and recognises them from a home she's plumbed. Even though she's sure they won't know her in her waders and raincoat and cap, still Phil keeps her face turned from the shore until they have gone.

'Scenery is wasted on a fisherman,' an old man told her once. 'A fisherman's world is only as long as the strength of his cast and deep as the seabed his lead finds,' he said, and Phil remembers thinking it was an oddly poetic thing to tell to a total stranger.

She doesn't bother preparing a new cod line and casting back out again. She knows it's pointless. She knows the sole line is even more pointless, still she leaves it to dabble in the shallows for another half hour. During many a long moment alone on a shoreline, Phil has made up a little song for almost every species, a kind of call which she pretends will summon whichever fish she means it for. Now she leans into the breakers and hums her sole refrain.

'Hmmm hmmm hm hm,' Phil hums, 'hhhmm hhhmm hm,' but the sound comes to nothing against the rushing and whooshing. She tries to smoke a cigarette and only when the rain has prevented her from lighting it for the tenth time does Phil finally reel in, repack her fishing box and head home.

Home is a tiny terrace house on the seafront of a village called Whitegate, a village which doesn't appear to have any white gates, or at least, none of prominence. Ever since Phil was a girl she's wanted to live in a house by the sea, but as a girl she never imagined there could be ugly, mundane places on the coast. There aren't any hanging baskets or promenades in Whitegate. There's a couple of warped picnic benches and a plastic ice-cream, tall as a child, chained to a streetlamp on the central embankment. The houses of the terrace are painted alternating shades of sepia as though frozen in time. The sewerage pipes jet watery shit straight out into the tide.

The storms continue into the following week. The amber warning is reduced to yellow but Phil doesn't notice any significant difference. Early on Tuesday morning as she is loading pumps and pipes into the back of her plumbing van, a red car pulls up on the seafront. The fogged-up window slides down to reveal a woman's face, bit by bit, beginning with the grey roots of curls, followed by skin the pallor of raw chicken, a chin, another chin. Even though she's stopped and rolled the window down, the woman keeps her engine lingering as she speaks.

'We lost our dog,' the woman says, 'on New Year's Eve, my fourteen-year-old is fierce upset.'

Phil nods, closes the door on her pumps and pipes and leans against the closed door to listen.

'Somebody down the way let off a firework right above our heads,' the woman says, 'and the dog just took off into the dark, flaking along. We're over in Ballinacurra and all day yesterday we searched the fields around our estate. Then late in the evening a neighbour said she saw a dog like him out along the main Ballinacurra-Whitegate road, so I came down first thing this morning.'

'I don't think I've seen a dog,' Phil says, 'what sort of dog?'

'A spaniel, a springer spaniel,' the woman's voice has gone squeaky with sorrow so she pauses to take a breath, to swallow. She looks very soberly at Phil and says: 'Do you think he'd have kept to the fields? Do you think he'd know to be sheltering in the hedges and that, what with all this weather?'

Phil doesn't know a thing about dogs. She thinks it strange that the woman would ask such a question. It's not that Phil is afraid or doesn't like them. It's not that she didn't beg her father for a puppy when she was a little girl. She isn't, she does, she did. She glances at the clock in her dashboard and thrums her fingertips against the glass as though she's pressed for time. She tells the

8

woman she doesn't know about dogs, she doesn't know whether they'd have the sense to shelter in hedges.

'But I'll keep an eye out,' she says, and it's only after the red car has disappeared down a side street that Phil realises she forgot to ask the woman for a contact number. She realises that even if she finds the springer spaniel, she won't have anyone to tell.

The next day Phil is called to look down a toilet in Ballinacurra. She hasn't driven the main road since Christmas, since before the storms began.

At the beginning of winter, the County Council sheared the ditches back to almost nothing. She presumed it was in preparation for widening, but it's two months now and still no roadworks have appeared. One day shortly after the cutting began, Phil noticed a jeep nosed into the hedge with its back doors open, and the man who owned the jeep was gathering the thickest branches severed by the County Council's mechanical slashers and piling them into his boot. The jeep's plate had a 2011 registration number and Phil wondered why a man with a relatively new and expensive vehicle needed to collect firewood from the side of the road. But over the course of the following few weeks, every time Phil passed that way there was a vehicle parked in a stretch of ditch, and sometimes they were jeeps and sometimes they were cars with trailers and sometimes they were just hatchbacks with the backseat, the passenger seat, even the baby seat all stacked high with damp sticks. Soon there were no severed branches left, big or small.

She finds the main road strewn with old leaves and crisp packets. Plastic bags and Christmas wrapping paper dangle from the shorn bushes and jostle in the wind. They catch in the corners of Phil's eyes as she drives, and every time, just for a split second, she thinks they're a dog. She thinks they are a white patch on a sheltering springer spaniel's coat.

*

In the Hope & Anchor, she tells the weeknight drinkers about the woman who lost her dog. No one has seen a spaniel but the man who rides on the back of the bin lorry says his neighbour's dog went missing a couple of weeks ago and hasn't turned up yet.

'The kiddies were walking it over the fields there,' he says, gesturing aimlessly toward the souvenir beer mugs hanging above the bar.

'It set after a rabbit or something. It had run off plenty times before only this time it hasn't come back again.'

'What sort of dog?' Phil asks.

'Like a small greyhound, what d'ya call them?'

One of the others helps him out by roaring WHIPPET, and the man who rides on the back of the bin lorry says it again, as though Phil is somehow unable to hear anybody in the pub but him.

'A whippet,' he says, 'that's what it was, a whippet.'

On the second Saturday of the new year, Phil makes a brown and white dinner for her father and herself. They eat it off their laps in the good front room. After they have both finished, Phil waits for her father to light a cigarette before following suit.

On the twenty-four-hour news station, there's a story about a thirty-nine-year-old man who strangled his mother, dismembered her body and dumped it beneath a hickory tree in his local nature reserve. She was discovered by a cyclist with rust-coloured dreadlocks, and as the cyclist enters and exits the courtroom he lifts his arms and spreads his fingers to shield his face as though he is the one to have done something wrong.

The weatherwoman comes next. From a chain around her neck swings a large blue stone and it bounces between her collarbones as she brandishes the pointer. Phil and her father watch in silence as the weatherwoman shows them how the huge band of low pressure causing the yellow storms will continue to hold its position for another week with no end in sight.

Out the good front room window, from the vantage of her straight-backed armchair, Phil notices how the cows have nibbled the grass down to practically nothing. When they raise their heads to moo she sees their front teeth are coated with mud. She looks at the nibbled ground and thinks of the main road with its ransacked ditches, the cliffs beyond the beach smashed and sucked away, the roll of toilet paper in the Hope & Anchor, and she feels very suddenly and very powerfully as though her world is dwindling away, morsel by morsel, without ever being replenished.

On Sunday, in place of the fine debris, there's a great crop of driftwood and plastic bottles running along the crest of the beach. Phil checks the bottles for messages. She doesn't find any. At the shoreline she turns to see how much of the cliff top has succumbed since last week. What used to be the crannies of nesting gulls are now mounds of wet mud on the rocks beneath. The expelled birds are weaving in the air above their buried homes and wistfully shrieking.

Again the beach is empty, except for Phil. She stays out for only an hour after last light. Although she cannot hear a thing above the shattering waves and shrieking gulls, still she hums the sole refrain, defiantly.

'Hmmm hmmm hm hm,' she hums, 'hhhmm hhhmm hm.'

She catches no sole, only a flounder she throws softly back across the waves like a skimming stone, and a whiting which she bakes in a coat of cheese and eats out of an oven dish standing at the kitchen counter late at night. As Phil eats, she examines her tide tables for the week. The spring tides are coming and she knows with all the rain and run-off and prevailing south-westerlies that the ground floor of her house will almost certainly flood.

At half past nine on Sunday night Phil clatters her oven dish into the sink and begins to clear her belongings from the kitchen floor. Doormat, vegetable bucket, rubbish bins, sweeping brush, pan, rug.

Phil learned to fish from a stranger called Alan Wrangles who published a book, *The Complete Guide to Sea Angling,* in the year she was born, as though he knew. She's still learning from the internet's inexhaustible community of like-minded strangers. Each night before bedtime she logs on to an angling forum and sits up for an hour with the laptop propped against her knees atop the duvet. She reads about what other anglers have caught and how and where, and she posts her own triumphs and flops, her tricks and spots. She doesn't mention the little bidding songs. She doesn't mention she's a woman. Whenever she photographs a fish she's caught lying on the sand beside her measure, she always crops away her woman's hand in Photoshop before posting it. Her username is solesearcher1, and for her profile picture, Phil uses an image she found online, a close-up of the bulbous, sidewise eyeballs of a flatfish.

Alan Wrangles taught her, but it was Phil's father who first took her out to fish. It must have been a thousand Sundays ago, back when he still had dark hair enough for thick sideburns. He only brought little Phil along because her mother was in hospital and she was yet too young to be left alone. On the beach, Phil Snr presented his daughter with his daintiest rod and showed her how to bait the hook, to cast. He seemed almost annoyed when she mastered it immediately.

Then Phil caught a flatfish in the shallows. It was tiny, the size of a hen's egg but mottled like a wren's. It lay flopping on the sand but it trained its squinted stare on Phil. She called her father over, but with her father came some stranger's loose dog, a great blundering mongrel which seized the fish and crunched and gulped. Then her father kicked the jaw which seized Phil's fish, and so the mongrel bit the foot which kicked its jaw and wouldn't let go until it punctured his boot and tasted blood.

Phil's mother never came out of hospital, and her father never went fishing again. His sideburns thinned until he'd only a few feathery strands combed across his crown, and not for many years after did he finally stop limping, and not until after he'd finally stopped limping did Phil start buying her own gear and driving to the beach alone. Years passed before she thought to look up the species of flatfish she'd reeled in that day. It was her first catch: a Dover sole.

All week, as the weatherwoman promised, the storms continue. Yellow, amber, orange, red; it doesn't matter what colour they are any more, their persistence is record-breaking. All week, Phil drives her plumbing van up and down the main road to the job in Ballinacurra which started with a blocked toilet and deteriorated into a whole system replacement. Every time she studies the gnarled undergrowth either side, and every time she mistakes a wilted sheet of wrapping paper for a cowering animal.

In the shop on Thursday morning, Phil's eyes stray to the community notice board. She takes a closer look, thinking that perhaps the woman in the red car who lost her spaniel will have pinned a sign up. Instead Phil finds two different appeals for missing dogs. One looks like the whippet mentioned in the Hope & Anchor, the other is a westie called Zimmo and the caption reads PLEASE HELP ME FIND MY WAY BACK HOME as though Zimmo himself had written it, and carried it here in his mouth, and asked the shop girl's permission to pin it up, and then went away again, to resume being lost.

*

The Ballinacurra job is almost finished by knocking-off time on Friday, and because Phil desperately doesn't want to return the following week, she decides to stay late and drives home through the dense dark listening to the squishing of her empty stomach. It's chucking rain and the high south-westerlies unrelentingly buffet the plumbing van. Phil is bone-weary from the week gone by. Her attention coasts from the cat's eyes to the ransacked ditches. This is stupid, she tells herself, they aren't even yours. Still she worries about all the lost dogs outside on their own in such stormy weather.

Rain squalls against the windscreen, the wipers throttle to and fro. It's so hard to see, and she almost doesn't manage to swerve in time to miss a man walking along the edge of the road. He has no high-visibility vest on, not even a luminous armband. It's almost as if the man is daring the oncoming traffic to hit him. He raises his arms and spreads his fingers in a way that reminds her of the rusted cyclist who found a dismembered mother beneath a hickory tree. Still Phil sees his face for long enough to recognise her father.

'What the fuck's he doing?' she says out loud to no one. Phil feels as though she should stop and turn around and go back for him, but she doesn't.

She continues to drive until she reaches the village. She parks alongside the central embankment where the ground is higher. On the opposite side of the road where she normally parks, the tide is rising through the drains and drowning the footpath in front of the terrace. The plastic ice-cream has been blown free of its chain and is bobbing. Phil fully expects to find the sea in her kitchen, but there is no sign of it, not yet.

On the third Saturday of the new year, the cows are at their loudest. They mistake Phil's van for the farmer's and stampede altogether to the edge of her father's garden and loiter behind the fence and bellow so hard they seem about to hyperventilate.

Neither Phil nor her father mentions what happened the previous night. After dinner they sit together in the good front room and smoke and watch the weatherwoman switching her pointer. She tells them the storm will endure for one more day and then, at last, conditions will begin to improve. She wears a wide-collared dress with a scarlet belt and Phil's father passes comment that she is fat, something he has never said before. Above the sound of the television and the cows, Phil thinks that she can hear the sound of a barking dog.

'It's coming from across the fields,' her father says, 'the farmer has a couple of scent hounds.'

On an ordinary Saturday, Phil would have asked why he doesn't phone the farmer and tell him the cows need to be fed, or rotated, or brought inside. But this Saturday, she doesn't say anything.

One more day of storms left, the only day of the week which matters, Sunday. Phil packs her fishing box and drives to the beach. The sand is covered with cornsilk-coloured scum. It lies in lines like piped cream; it wheels along the strand. She puts out two rods. One for something she might actually catch, and one for Dover sole.

Today, she doesn't hum, she has no appetite for humming. Both her lines collect eelgrass faster than she can clear them. The eelgrass slaps the wind and drags down the rods, the stand. Phil splashes into the scum, begins to wade out and out and out after her gear, but today there's no comfort in the squeeze of the sea. The waves are too big. They ram against her shoulders, her chest. She turns her face down and sees nothing but spew. She sees nothing but spew and still she thinks she can discern tiny flatfish at her feet, lying down and staring upwards. But the waves break into her eyes and splash up her nose and force her back.

On the beach, there is a man standing where just a moment ago, there was no man. His raincoat is a yellow beacon against the blackened sky. He comes into the water to meet her. He stretches out his arms and helps Phil in.

'I was watching from the cliff,' he says, 'I've been watching all week now, I've been keeping a look out for my…'

'Your dog,' Phil says. 'You've lost your dog.'

'How did you know?' The man says.

'Because I know,' Phil says. 'I know where your dog is.'

She drives fast. She hopes the stranger from the beach can keep up in his car behind her. She hopes he can keep up but she doesn't slow down; she can't slow down. By the time Phil reaches her father's house, the stranger's headlamps have vanished from her rear-view mirror.

Phil Snr must have heard her van coming up the boreen. He is standing outside his bungalow, on the asphalt in the rain with the cows all lined up behind him like an unsaddled cavalry. Phil pushes past her father and stumbles toward the back side of the house. She rounds the wheelie bin, ducks under the washing line and crosses the lawn. Even before she's reached the coal bunker, she knows she is right.

She slides the bolt and pulls. She covers her mouth with the sleeve of her oilskin. The smell is worse than silage and sewerage and the guts lorry in summer. All Phil can see from the door is the white tip of a tail, and it is wagging very slowly as the blackened light falls in.

She looks away and sees her father has followed and is standing on the grass a few yards from the bunker, the gales blowing his feathery hair up, the rain streaming down his hairless pate.

'Be sure and shut the door now,' he says to his daughter.

And when Phil fails to react he says it again; he shouts it over the wind and cows.

*

Come the evening tide, the kitchen finally begins to flood. Phil is sitting at the table in her waders, and there are sandbags piled on the back step but now she sees for the first time that the water doesn't leak in through the door but rises from between the floor tiles. She sits at the table in her waders and watches as the room slowly fills up with sea. She smokes cigarette after cigarette and thinks about how it is her job to make water come, and now the water's coming and she's the solitary passenger of a sinking ship.

But of course the tide goes out again. Inch by inch, the sea dribbles back into the fissures it rose from, until there's nothing but a cloudy puddle in the dip of the back door step. Through a blur of cigarette smoke, just for a second, Phil thinks she can see something flopping in the puddle. Something the size of a hen's egg but mottled like a wren's, something miraculous.

But as the smoke clears Phil sees it's only the muck of her kitchen floor collected by the floodwater and shaped into the ghost of a tiny flatfish.

And at last, she gets up, opens the door, lets the last of the sea out and watches her sole disperse back into dirt.

Go Down Sunday

Trevor Byrne

Judges' Comments

'Go Down Sunday', the story of a boy's football team on a week away in small-town Ireland, is an absorbing tale about the moments in which boyhood crack open towards adolescence; the excitement of independence, the ease with which home is left behind. The story has a dark heart, and the reader is manipulated with the same ease as the main character; we are left, as in the best stories, with troubling questions.

Author's Note

The rough guts of this story were thrashed out in Manchester, and I returned to it a year later in a hostel in London (the story is set in a hostel in Arklow in the 1980s). I was staying in Hackney for a long weekend with a dozen bands I know from Ireland. Each morning I got up at five and wrote in a dark corner while the others drank and laughed and howled. On the ferry to Dublin on the Monday these same lads slept and groaned and turned pale green while I wrote.

I wrote, in the end, a story which features a priest but isn't, I don't think, about priests, or the Church or God. The story is about being young and lonely and clever, though perhaps not clever enough. Or not yet wise enough, anyhow; not when matched against someone attractive and devious and older. The story's central relationship, between a boy and a priest, is skewed and spooky and probably ruinous. The two main characters—Stephen and Father Larkin—appear, some twenty years later, in a novel I'm currently working on.

—*Trevor Byrne*

STEPHEN PEELED THE SHORTS from his hip and saw that it was nothing; there was some blood but hardly any, just enough to gum the underpants under his shorts to his skin.

He leaned against the wall to catch his breath and watch the others, the ball skidding about the yard and the lads chasing and hustling, squinting against the low sun and the swirling dust. He waited, then just as James Swann was about to pass him, Stephen sprang from the wall and blindsided him, kicking the ball from James's foot just as he was about to shoot.

—Slydog! James shouted, and he whooped and laughed. The loose ball came back off the gates and Thomas Farrell caught it first time, a snapshot from a mad angle with his left foot which Declan Cope charged down, sending the ball skidding up the yard. It was an improvised, lawless mess of a game, and Stephen was laughing now too, laughing at everything and nothing, at the fact that they were all here together, miles from home.

The oldest player on the team was Terry McDonagh, who was fourteen, and eight minutes older than Shay McDonagh, his twin. Stephen was the third youngest of the sixteen; he was thirteen and two months. St Mark's Football Club were a good team, and they were in Arklow as a reward for finishing second in their schoolboys' league. Stephen, like most of the lads, had never been out of Dublin before, and they were playing now to keep exhaustion at bay, playing at a peak of energy and emotion at the ending of a long day of excitement and travel.

As it began to cool the lads grew quiet and the game became more intense and intricate; they were hard in their tackles and Stephen's hip and ankles were raw and thrumming after a dozen kicks. Stephen hadn't a clue what score it was or who was winning or if it was even possible to win, but none of that mattered: he was exhausted, but at the same time he was endlessly awake and endlessly alive, and he didn't miss Dublin or the house or his mother.

Soon it became hard to see the ball, but even so they'd have played on only a country man with sideburns came and rattled the gate and shouted at them, told them there were people living above the shops across the way and they'd a baby that was trying to sleep, or did they not sleep in Dublin these days, was sleep too uncool for them in the city?

—Sorry, said Stephen. He rolled the ball onto his foot and balanced it, then flicked it lightly to Thomas Farrell, their captain, who caught it and held it to his chest. The man muttered and walked away into the dark.

—Sleep is for sheep, said James Swann, when it was safe, and the lads laughed. Stephen laughed too, at how stupid a thing it was to say, and then he turned back to the hostel and he saw Father Larkin leaning against the doorframe, watching them.

—We're havin' a meeting, a team meetin', now, said Paddy Conroy, and he led them into what the lads were calling the mess hall. Paddy Conroy was the manager of St Mark's FC. He'd driven the bus to Arklow and he was annoyed as usual. Paddy and Dillon Clarke, the young assistant manager, took up position at the end of the room, their backs to a long window and the deepening blue of the country summer at night. Paddy was a tall, thin, balding man who the lads considered to be ancient and clueless; they all preferred Dillon, who was much younger and had had trials in England when he was only a little older than the lads were now. That Manchester United didn't offer him professional terms in the end, and that his career in the League of Ireland with Shelbourne was ended when he was only nineteen after he wrecked his cruciate ligament, didn't matter to the lads: Dillon was the closest any of them had ever been to a real footballer and he had their respect.

Father Larkin was sitting to the right of Paddy on a shabby sunken armchair, sitting easily and relaxed, as though the mess hall was a better place than it really was. He was a young priest and many of the girls at school fancied him. Father Larkin had lived in New York and he spoke with a slight American accent, and Stephen wondered if that was where he'd been since he'd seen him last, over a year ago. He didn't think Father Larkin was anything to do with St Mark's FC, but he was very glad to see him.

—Okay, shut up now, listen, said Paddy, and the lads quietened down. —These are the laws of the land, yeah? First off, no more football is to be played in the yard, we're only here two hours and you have a ball scuffed to bits. If you want to play ball in the yard you can get a plastic ball in the town.

Paddy held up the ball they'd been playing with.

—The leather's ruined on that now, look, it's all flappin' off, he said. —That was only brand new. We're not made of leather footballs. And here, no one's to be sittin' on balls either, especially you Terry, with that bleedin' arse on you, they'll all be gone egg-shaped.

The lads laughed and Terry told them to fuck off.

—Duck arse, said James Swann, after they quietened down, and they laughed again.

—Leave it out, mallet head, said Paddy.

He then went on to lay out the rest of the laws of the land: dinner was whenever, they'd see how it went, but breakfast was always at nine and everyone was to be ready for it; after ten o'clock at night was quiet time; no one was to go beyond the gates no matter what time it was, unless they were with someone and they had permission first off Paddy or Dillon. Lastly, there was to be no acting the maggot, a vague rule which gave Paddy plenty of power.

Paddy looked at Father Larkin, to see if that was everything, and then remembered something else. —And no touchin' anyone's stuff, he said. —If there's any vandalism of personal property, or robbin' or anything like that, especially robbin', you're off home, back to Dublin. No second chances.

—It's miles to Dublin, said Thomas Quinn.

—You'll be escorted back on the train with Dillon.

Stephen looked quickly at Dillon and saw him smile and shake his head, though he said nothing. Stephen liked looking at people's faces, at what they did with their hands.

—Before you hit the hay, said Father Larkin, standing, —I just want to offer my congratulations on a great season. Next time you'll go one better and win it, I'm convinced.

The lads cheered and clapped, and Father Larkin said goodnight and God bless, and left, smiling.

He could hear James, behind him, brushing his teeth, and it seemed to Stephen he took forever; already he'd been brushing for double the time Stephen did at home.

Stephen was sitting by the window of the room he was sharing with James, watching the night sky. He had borrowed a book about astronomy from the library earlier that summer and he could see the stars the book showed much more clearly here than in Dublin, where often he could see nothing at all. There were specks of light, mostly white but sometimes with hints of yellow or orange, everywhere in the black sky. The roofs of the shops across the way were almost the same black as the sky. In front of the shops a light come on in one of the parked cars, and he saw that it was Father Larkin's car, an expensive car which the lads had admired at school last year.

Stephen stepped back from the window and rubbed his stinging hip. James said something with his gob full of spitty toothpaste.

—I can't hear what you're sayin', said Stephen.

James spat the froth into the little sink and wiped his mouth with his hand. —I said, this toothpaste is nice.

Stephen was a long time lying in the dark. It was very warm and he wished he'd opened the ceiling window before getting into bed and turning off the light.

After the football in the yard Stephen had felt awake and elated, they all had, and they'd fallen into the sofas and armchairs in the mess hall excitedly chatting and bantering, but soon the mood changed and they became tired. Stephen felt the tiredness too, a kind of liquidy, melting tiredness, but now he was restless again and couldn't get to sleep: he'd been sitting by the window for ages before the light came on in the car, and he kept thinking of Father Larkin sitting alone in the dark for all that time.

Stephen woke early and it was already bright. In the other bed James Swann was breathing through his mouth and his pale legs were showing. Stephen took up his kitbag and left quietly and dressed in the big communal toilets. He looked at himself in the mirror and pushed his hair about.

There was no one downstairs, but he was still careful to open the door without making any noise. There was no wind and it was hot. Stephen walked across the yard and hopped the gate and walked the length of the street. The only place open was a café called Downey's.

—Morning, said a girl behind the counter, when Stephen stepped in. She was a little older than Stephen, and had short blonde hair and was wearing hoop earrings. Stephen looked around at the empty chairs and tables.

—Do I sit down or go up to you or what do I do? he said.

—Take a seat and I'll be down to you, said the girl, and he thought the country accent sounded nice coming from her, unlike the man with the sideburns who'd given out to them the night before.

Stephen took the table by the window. He looked up at the girl, then wiped his palm across the tabletop: it was warm. When the girl was making her way to his table he noticed that she was wearing flat shoes, so thin that it sounded as though she was barefoot.

—What'll you have, so?

—Tea, just, said Stephen. He hadn't the money to get the breakfast on the menu, but tea was grand, he liked tea. In a few minutes the girl brought him a shiny steel pot and a cup and milk, and he felt good making the tea and drinking it in the morning sun. He was careful and made it last.

Stephen had almost finished when a man with an *Irish Times* under his arm came in and sat at the next table. He ignored Stephen and placed his folded newspaper at an angle against the small vase of flowers, so he could read it when his breakfast came. The man had white, thick hair and eyebrows that stuck out from his head. He was wearing a light windbreaker and, underneath it, a suit jacket, shirt and tie. When the girl came with her notepad the man asked for a scotch egg and a glass of red wine.

Facing the hostel there was a shop called J Wilkinson's Electrical

Contractor. Up above the shop there were two windows with net curtains, and in the ground floor window display there was a red fan and electric kettles and small heaters and lamps and hoovers, and among them many dead flies and moths, dried out and hollow.

Inside, the shop was small and hot and very cluttered. The man who'd given out to them at the gate the night before was behind the counter, reading a newspaper. He didn't look up at Stephen.

Stephen wandered the cluttered aisles, picking things up and looking at them, and he wondered why anyone would want to own a shop like this, which seemed to him more like a warehouse. The man behind the counter didn't care about the shop, or else it wouldn't be so dirty and disorderly. If Stephen owned the shop he'd have a radio playing to break the silence.

He couldn't find the red fan on any of the shelves, so he went to the counter. The man's sideburns mixed in with his wiry black hair, and he was wearing a plaid shirt with the top few buttons open and the sleeves rolled up. Stephen could see more dark hair on the man's chest and arms.

—How much are your fans?

The man finished reading his sentence or pretended to, then looked at Stephen.

—Which one?

Stephen hadn't seen any other fans besides the red one. —That one, he said, pointing at it.

—A fiver for that one, said the man.

A fiver was half Stephen's money.

—Do you not have a box for it?

—I can put it in a box.

The man turned on his stool and started to rummage through the boxes behind him. He picked up a brown cardboard box.

—I don't want that one.

—What's wrong with that box?

—It'll look cheap in that.

—You'll have the receipt with the price on it.

Stephen didn't want a new fan in an old box, that would ruin it.
—Is there not one with a picture of the fan on it? The real box?

—I've ones in the boxes upstairs, said the man. —I'd have to root them out though.

—If you've a new one in a box I'll buy it off you during the week.

The man stared at him but Stephen didn't look away.

—You're from across the road, one of the Dublin boys.

Stephen nodded.

—Keep the fuckin' noise down, said the man.

—What time have you? Father Larkin was saying to Dillon Clarke, as Stephen stepped into the mess hall. Dillon was sitting on the arm of the red sofa, wearing a tracksuit.

Dillon looked at his watch. —Twenty-five past eight, he said. Then he looked at Stephen. —Where were you?

—Just down the end of the yard, said Stephen.

—It's a stunning morning, said Father Larkin. —Out is the place to be alright.

Paddy came in, rubbing his cheek. His eyes were red and seemed to have shrunk in the night.

—Mornin', men, he said.

—Good morning, Mr Conroy, said Father Larkin. —We were just discussing time.

—Time? What? said Paddy.

—You know, I've had this watch for almost twenty years and it's still perfect, said Father Larkin. He held out his wrist to Stephen. —Have a proper look at that, Stephen, he said, and Stephen was surprised and pleased that Father Larkin remembered his name and had used it so easily. —Here, look, you can't judge something's worth from a mile away.

Father Larkin wore the watch with the face on the underside of his wrist, which was something Stephen had never seen before; he had to turn his arm to show Stephen. The watch was gold and plain, with a large face and a thick dark leather strap. Father Larkin's arm was paler on the underside.

—My father gave me this watch before he died. He bought it in Antwerp, in Belgium, as a gift to himself, the first good thing he ever bought himself.

—A hairloom, said Paddy, and Father Larkin glanced at Stephen. Stephen knew that Paddy had made a mistake. He smiled. Paddy was oblivious: he was pulling things out of the presses.

—We'll make the breakfast for nine o' clock, Dillon, he said. —Yeah?

—Sound, yeah, said Dillon. —We should get them on the run way before eleven or it'll be too hot. And we've the pool tournament tonight as well, remember.

—Tonight? said Paddy.

—Yeah, tonight.

—We have an accomplished snooker player in our midst, said Father Larkin.

—Who? Stephen? said Paddy.

—Stephen Sheridan, the very man, said Father Larkin.

Stephen was smiling; Father Larkin had remembered what he'd told him.

Stephen first met Father Larkin, though only briefly, a year before when Father Larkin took their Religion class for a day when Father O'Malley was sick. Some of the girls said that Father Larkin was a ride, but others didn't like him because he made them do proper work, which they weren't used to, as Father O'Malley was old and bewildered and let them do what they wanted. Father Larkin made them get into groups and talk about people's rights, and what we should and shouldn't be allowed to do if God gave us free will. Father Larkin sat in on the groups for a few minutes each, and when Stephen said —If you do something that takes someone else's rights away then that's wrong, Father Larkin said, —Exactly. Very good, and smiled.

Father O'Malley was better by the next class and it was another month before Stephen saw Father Larkin again. He had the use of Father O'Malley's little office for a few days so he could speak with some of the students, about anything that was on their minds. Stephen didn't go to Mass or think much about God, nor did he want to, but he thought it would be good to talk to Father Larkin again, and the next day he was in Father O'Malley's office.

Father Larkin shook Stephen's hand, and Stephen sat in front of the desk, which was piled with newspapers and old copybooks. The walls were cement blocks painted yellow.

The first thing Father Larkin said was, —Do you know what psychology is, Stephen?

Stephen had heard the word but he didn't know exactly what it meant, not well enough to say anything.

—Don't worry, Stephen. I'm not a teacher, this isn't a test.

—Okay, said Stephen, but he thought probably he had failed a test of some kind, and he felt annoyed that Father Larkin had come at him in that way.

—In fact I know you know what it means, it's probably just the word that's unfamiliar to you. Psychology is what you think, which isn't always the same as what you say. Psychology is your thoughts and the things that go on in your head.

—Like what a psychiatrist does or something, said Stephen.

—Exactly. A psychiatrist is similar except they dole out

medication. A psychologist just talks to you about your thoughts, the same as a priest does. Sometimes they don't talk at all, they're just quiet, and the person they're working with does all the talking. You might be thinking something or worrying about something, and you wouldn't even know.

Stephen nodded.

—I know what you're really thinking, Stephen.

Stephen looked away, as Father Larkin was looking at him very closely. He looked at the wall, as though there was something interesting there, when in fact there was nothing interesting about it at all, it was just concrete blocks painted yellow. He knew it was his turn to say something, but he couldn't think of anything.

—It's okay to be quiet, you know, said Father Larkin, after a few moments of silence. —It's largely a performance with the rest of them in your class, they all try to outdo each other. That's the psychologist in me speaking. All the shouting, you know, the acting out, all this running around like crazy people. That's all acting. And in a way that's all fine of course, but I think a dose of honesty is healthy, and a dose of maturity. You're very honest, Stephen. You don't have to speak to be honest, but you need honesty to be friends with someone.

Stephen nodded. He'd already nodded too much. He felt nervous but he was excited too.

—Are you from America? said Stephen.

—No, I'm from here, Dublin. My parents still live in Blackrock. But I spent almost eight years in a parish in Boston.

—Do you miss Boston?

—Sometimes, sure. But Dublin's good too. Dublin's still home.

They spoke in the office for half an hour, which was as long as Stephen was allowed to miss class. Stephen told Father Larkin about the things he liked – football, and space a bit, but especially snooker – and Father Larkin said that those were excellent interests. Stephen surprised himself with the amount of talking he did once he got going: he told Father Larkin that his father didn't live with them anymore, and that Paul, his brother, was in jail. Father Larkin asked if Paul was messing with drugs and Stephen said he didn't know but that he might be. He told Father Larkin that Paul was locked up for taking a sledgehammer to a car that was parked in an industrial estate. Stephen thought it was a mad, savage thing to do, to just wreck the car, not even to try to rob it. But maybe robbing cars wasn't exciting or interesting to Paul.

—Do you attend Mass, Stephen? asked Father Larkin.

—Not much.

Stephen's mother wasn't pushed about Mass; she didn't go herself, not even at Christmas. For a while his mother made Paul bring Stephen to Mass on Sunday mornings, but after Paul began to bring him to the Gala, the local snooker hall, instead, she gave up. Stephen still went alone to the Gala most Sundays and loved stepping from the light and the noise of the street into the dark hall. The darkness in the Gala was a different kind, it wasn't bedroom dark, the darkness you woke to at night, or the electric dark behind your eyes when you closed them tightly; the dark in the hall was calm, it was a dark that didn't hold its breath but breathed slowly and deeply. He loved the low ceiling and the blue chalk dust. Most of all he loved the tables, their scale and weight, the smoothness glowing beneath the hanging lights. It was a quiet and serious place, the quiet broken now and then by a laugh or a whistle in recognition of something miraculous, something ingenious or lucky or both.

When Stephen was leaving Father Larkin stood up too and stepped out from behind the desk. He was taller than Stephen by a foot or so.

—You're doing well, Stephen, and I'll help you, he said.

Father Larkin adjusted the collar of Stephen's uniform jumper.

*

Stephen was surprised that the hall was bigger than the Gala, given how small a town Arklow was, but for all that the place was massive there were only two snooker tables: it was a pool hall, really.

They were supposed to play a pool tournament but Paddy quickly became stressed and annoyed trying to keep track of things, and he told the lads to just play away. Paddy and Dillon played on one of the snooker tables, and the other was already being played on by two local men who placed their pints on the table when they were taking their shot, so that one of them had to quickly lift his off when the balls bounced in an unexpected way, which was almost every time as they weren't good or serious players. Stephen tried to keep an eye on the table so he could claim it, but the drunk men left while he was taking a shot and Thomas Quinn and Declan Cope began racking the balls before he could do anything.

Stephen was playing doubles. As usual his partner was James Swann, and they were playing against the McDonagh twins. The game was dragging on: James wasn't taking it seriously, he kept talking about football and each time it was his shot he was surprised and had to be told what colour he was on, or he'd ask Stephen which shot he should go for, and then he'd take the shot and miss and start talking again.

Thomas Quinn and Declan Cope, on the snooker table, weren't playing properly either: they weren't keeping score and it'd take them all day to finish a frame. Father Larkin was watching them, leaning against the wall with his arms folded, smoking. Declan Cope went for a long black without potting a red first, and when the ball dropped into the pocket he held the cue over his head and shouted out —Jimmy White!

Father Larkin stubbed out the cigarette and stepped into the light and took the black ball from the pocket. —Foul, he said, and he untucked his shirt and rubbed the ball and put in on its spot. Father Larkin told Thomas and Declan that he'd referee for them. He said playing pool on a snooker table was like pro wrestlers trying to dance ballet.

Stephen laughed. He hadn't meant to, and Father Larkin looked at him and Stephen looked away, as though he was more interested in his wreck of a game with James against the McDonaghs. When he looked back Father Larkin was still watching him.

—Thomas to break, said Father Larkin, but when Thomas leaned casually into his break-off shot Father Larkin tapped the rail and shook his head. —That's all wrong, he said. —Okay, stay as you are. He leaned over Thomas and reached back and adjusted Thomas's grip, and together they sized up the shot.

—You sight along the cue, said Father Larkin. —Hold your head still, don't lift it till you're done. Get your chin right on the cue. You ever see these guys with cleft chins, these movie guys? They get that from playing snooker, from the cue rubbing against their chin. Which red is he after, Stephen?

He said this last without looking up from the table. Stephen pointed at the corner red at the back of the pack.

Thomas took the shot but there was too little power in it and the reds no more than jostled and none came away from the pack.

—Foul break, said Stephen.

—Ah here, said Thomas. He was exasperated and bored already.

They played a few more shots, with Father Larkin coaching them, showing them how to cue properly and which ball to play for and which side of the ball to hit, before Declan said snooker was pure brutal and Thomas agreed: it was gank, it was boring, it was too slow. Father Larkin joked with them and said that they'd learn but he let them go and they hurried off to one of the pool tables.

Stephen was standing at the end of the table waiting for Father
Larkin to ask if he wanted to play. He rolled the white back up the
table and straightened the reds, then came round to the baulk end
of the table and Father Larkin put his hand on Stephen's shoulder.

—I'll break, said Father Larkin, smiling. He clipped the red at
the back of the bunch and knocked a few reds free, but the white
only came back as far as the blue.

—What do you think?

—Good, said Stephen.

—Come on, honestly. We're looking at the same table.

—The white's a bit short, he said, and he felt his face redden.

—This guy's a professional in the making, said Father Larkin to
Dillon and Paddy. Paddy looked up from his shot and raised his
eyebrows and squinted and nodded vaguely, then lowered his
head, and Stephen saw the shine of his red scalp through the thin,
cobwebby hair.

—You're up, said Father Larkin.

Stephen sized up one of the reds and potted it handily into the
bottom right pocket and left himself with an easy black. He didn't
look up at Father Larkin but he knew the priest was looking at
him. He potted the black but he ran too far and wasn't on the next
red as he'd planned it, and he sized it up anyway and tried for the
middle left pocket. He missed but he hadn't left any easy pots on.

Father Larkin missed the red. —I'm in for a real battle here, he
said.

It was a battle and it was close but Father Larkin won. Some of
the lads stood around the table as they played. Father Larkin
challenged Stephen to best out of three, and Stephen won the
second frame and again it was close, and they started the decider.
Father Larkin knew about snooker: he knew that Stephen Hendry,
Stephen's favourite player, had won the UK Championships that
year, and he said he'd seen Alex Higgins play pool in New York in

an exhibition and had met him afterwards. Stephen was playing well and his nerves were good and he felt happy, but Dillon Clarke came to their table and told them to wind up halfway through the frame. There was a moment when Stephen thought Father Larkin was going to say they were staying on the table until they finished, and Stephen felt he probably did have the authority to do that, even though he wasn't part of the football team.

—That's okay, said Father Larkin. —We'll have to come back and finish this during the week. This is a grudge match.

It was late in the evening when they left the hall but it was still bright and busy outside and Arklow seemed a very beautiful place to Stephen. The lads were loud and full of energy; James Swann climbed halfway up a lamp post before Paddy Conroy saw him and shouted at him, and he slid down like a fireman on a pole.

—We're stoppin' at the chipper, said Paddy, and the lads shouted what they wanted: burgers and smoked cod and the likes, but Paddy told them it was too complicated to take a big order like that, he'd get eight singles of chips to share, and a battered sausage for each of them. Paddy and Dillon went into the chipper and ordered the food and the lads waited outside with Father Larkin, who asked them who was rooming with who: he pointed to Adam Roache and said, —Right, so it's Adam and... ? and Adam said, —I'm with Thomas, and then he asked another lad, Fran Walsh, who said he was with Dean Prendergast, and then he asked Stephen who he was sharing with.

—James Swann, said Stephen.

—James Swann, very good, said Father Larkin. He didn't ask any more of the lads who they were rooming with, though they started shouting names at him anyway, the names of girls from school, Hulk Hogan, Mikhail Gorbachev.

*

36

The next day they were brought to the seafront to fish for sea bass. As with everything else the outing was based around Paddy Conroy's interests and what he thought would be easiest to organise and supervise. Dillon Clarke came too but Father Larkin had to go off somewhere in his car.

Paddy had brought three fishing rods with him to Arklow and the plan was to cast off from the pier and for the lads to take turns with the two smaller rods while Paddy did the real fishing.

The outing was a shambles: the lads messed about and argued while Paddy cast out and from time to time turned his head and complained or shouted at them, or chastised Dillon, telling him he wasn't cut out for youth work. Someone had torn the the picture of a topless woman from a newspaper and it was passed around until it was caught by the wind and ended up in the sea. Soon the two fishing lines were twined together and Paddy called the whole thing off.

Earlier, Father Larkin had suggested that they all try to stay off meat today, seeing as it was a Friday and they were going fishing. Shay McDonagh reminded Paddy of this and said he'd have to pay for smoked cods for them now.

—You can go down to the beach and get yourself a bucket of winkles if you want to eat seafood, said Paddy, and in the end they had the usual: chips and battered sausages, but this time with curry sauce as well. Paddy too had his usual and sat at the kitchen table with a piece of fried fish and a heap of chips on the greasy paper in front of him. He ate the fish with his hands: dipped the pieces of fish in their batter into a tub of curry sauce then stuffed them into his his mouth and had no shame at all in his ugly way of eating.

Stephen was drying the dishes when Father Larkin came in and took a cup from the press and filled it with milk. He wasn't wearing his collar and Stephen thought that without the collar you wouldn't think he was a priest at all.

—What did you think of that magazine, Stephen? said Father Larkin, and he took a sip of his milk.

Stephen said nothing. It embarrassed him when the lads spoke about girls but an adult saying it was worse.

—You did see it, I presume?

Stephen's face was hot. He wished Father Larkin would stop, he was ruining everything now.

—Sexuality is a part of life, Stephen, he said, and he came to the sink and looked at Stephen, smiling. —I'm levelling with you here. But I can see I'm embarrassing you, so let's leave it at that.

Stephen could hear the lads shouting and laughing in the mess hall. He and Father Larkin stood for a few moments in silence, and then Dillon Clarke stepped into the kitchen.

—How you gettin' on, Stephen? he said.

—Grand, I'm nearly finished.

—Give me a shout if you need one of the lads to help, he said. He looked from Stephen to Father Larkin, then went back to the mess hall. Stephen heard Dillon clapping his hands and telling James Swann to get down off of the sofa before he fell out the window.

—They're a lively crew, said Father Larkin. —Wrecking the place and magazines and all that sort of thing, it's understandable for boys your age.

Father Larkin took another sip of milk. Stephen wanted to say something, to speak to Father Larkin as he'd done so easily before at school. Stephen's parents and Paul and Paddy Conroy knew nothing about the world, and nothing about Stephen. The only one who was any use was Dillon Clarke, but unlike Father Larkin, Dillon had time for everyone, even hyper eejits like James Swann.

—It wasn't a magazine, it was the girl in *The Sun*, said Stephen.
—She has clothes on her, just no top.

—Well, that's a distinction worth making. Declan Cope said it was a full magazine.

—He's just talking, he doesn't even know. He hasn't a clue about anything.

It was almost ten o' clock but it was still bright. Stephen told James Swann that he was going for a walk and James said he'd come with him, but Stephen wanted to go on his own.

As he walked along the sloping seafront street he saw the beach and the sea in dappled flashes through the trees, and it seemed that there were people there, standing still and watching the water, but when he finally had a clear view, as he made his way down the wide stone steps to the sand, he saw that the people were stones, and he pressed his palms against them, stones his own height and taller partway buried and tapering at angles towards the sky. They were two different types, either slick and smooth and covered with a green skin or dry and pocked like the inside of a teapot.

Stephen took off his runners and carried them, and he liked the feel of the wet sand tightly packed beneath his bare feet. He walked until the dark of the sea and the sky were almost the same kind, and he came to a tugboat sunk into the sand, the paint flaking from the rusted hull. He'd have liked to have looked in the cabin but there was no clear way to get up to the deck: there was a scrap of rusted ladder bolted to the hull but it was too high up.

It was fully dark by the time he walked back to the stone steps and the sloping street. Up ahead the lights of a car cut the dark. Stephen stepped behind a tree and crouched there and the car passed, and when he got back to the hostel he threw pebbles at the window until James looked out.

—Where'd you go? said James, when he opened the front door.

—Just down the beach. There's a boat I found, a wreck. It'd be good to try to get into maybe.

They were on the stairs now. They went into their room.

—I had to tell that you'd gone out.

—Why?

—I was just sittin' here and yer man Father Larkin knocked on the door and looked in and said where were you and I said you were in the jacks but he didn't believe me. And anyway he could've checked easy. So I said you went for a walk but you wouldn't be long.

—So did he go out to look for me or something?

—I don't know. He went out in his car. He's probably gone home or wherever he goes.

The moon was pale up above in the skylight, and James was breathing loudly.

Stephen lay awake for a good long while. Probably he didn't go back to sleep at all, though he wasn't sure. It had been bright for a long time when he heard Paddy Conroy shouting from the hall:

—We're havin' a meeting, a team meetin', now.

The lads filed down the stairs into the mess hall. Stephen sloped down, last. Paddy and Dillon were standing as before, in front of the long window, though this time the yard outside was quiet and bright. Father Larkin wasn't there.

—Lads, I'm not gonna mess around here, I want this sorted, said Paddy. —Whoever took the watch, and they know who they are, would want to put it back right now.

—Whose watch? said Stephen.

—Father Larkin's watch, his golden watch. Now lads, that watch is expensive, it was given to Father Larkin by his da, years ago, so it's a family hairloom. I don't want to get the guards into this but I will if I have to, your mas and das will be called, the lot.

The lads were looking about, whispering, excited. They jokingly accused each other.

—I swear to God, lads, this is serious, said Paddy.

—How does he know someone robbed it? said Shay McDonagh.

—Could he not've just lost it? said Terry McDonagh.

—He didn't lose the bleedin' watch, said Paddy. —It's a pure golden watch, come on now.

Paddy kept saying that it was a golden watch and Father Larkin wouldn't lose a pure golden watch like that. He said golden as though the watch was magical; he should have just said gold. Father Larkin would have noticed it too, Stephen thought.

—Well, we don't know, he could've lost it, said Dillon. —Father Larkin's not sayin' it was definitely robbed, he's just sayin' it's missin'. Anyway, it doesn't matter one way or the other once it stops bein' missin', yeah?

—Now get up and get ready for this walk, said Paddy.

They were going to look at a quarry, then they'd be playing a few five-a-sides, concentrating on keep-ball.

—What's a quarry? asked James Swann.

—A big fuckin' hole, said Stephen.

Father Larkin came to the hostel after they'd seen the big hole, and explained to the lads that he was sure none of them had taken the watch. It must have come off somehow, slipped from his wrist; or else he'd put it down somewhere. It was from before waterproof watches were invented so he did take it off a lot.

After they'd eaten in the hostel, Father Larkin, with Paddy and Dillon, took the lads to see St Saviour's Church.

—It might be a bit of a fool's errand, trying to get you guys to think a church is cool, said Father Larkin, as they set out, —but we'll give it a go.

The lads and Paddy and Dillon wandered about the church grounds, and Stephen and Father Larkin went inside. Father Larkin was blessing himself with holy water from the marble font when James Swann came in behind them. Stephen and James blessed themselves with the water too, and James flicked some from his fingertips at Stephen.

They walked in silence along the left aisle, one behind the other, Father Larkin first and James last, each looking up at the high vaulted ceiling. Father Larkin passed a large, pale statue of a pained and hungered Jesus. James stopped and Father Larkin walked on.

—You'd think he'd miracle up a battered sausage or something, said James.

—He looks half dead, I hate statues like that, said Stephen.

Father Larkin waited for them at the back of the church. As Stephen and James reached him a heavy side door near the entrance opened and a young priest in vestments stepped out and closed the door quietly behind him. He stopped and bowed quickly, then walked directly towards them, the same way they'd come. The priest seemed to be thinking or remembering, and he was wearing large glasses which caught the sun through the stained-glass windows. He didn't acknowledge them at all and Stephen thought he'd walk straight past them into the little prayer room, but Father Larkin said, —Excuse me, and lifted his hand and the priest stopped suddenly, as though woken up. He looked at Father Larkin and then at Stephen and James. The young priest had round cheeks and blotched skin, and his eyes looked very large behind the big lenses. He looked to Stephen like Dennis Taylor, the snooker player, a younger version of him.

—Hi, said Father Larkin.

—Hello, said the priest.

—I've just been showing these young men around the church, it's beautiful.

—Oh it is. We're blessed to have such a beautiful building.

He sounded like Dennis Taylor, too.

—Could you give us a little history, Father?

—Oh, yes, yes, said the priest, though he looked around quickly first, and seemed flustered. —What would you like to know?

—The whole story, said Father Larkin, looking round and nodding. He caught Stephen's gaze momentarily, the way he had when Paddy Conroy said hairloom.

—Well, the whole story, you know, that'd be beyond me.

—Tell us what you know.

—Well, I can tell you that the church was built just before 1900, so it's almost a hundred years old. Which isn't that old really compared to some. It was built on the the back of a very kind and very substantial donation from… oh dear me. He paid for the bells too, an earl he was, and they're very fine bells, though I don't know too much about them. We get bell ringers coming to us from all over the place, from England. They have clubs, these bell-ringing clubs.

Father Larkin nodded. —It's a storied little town, he said.

—Oh yes, it is.

The priest looked past them. He was scratching his shoulder slowly.

—Of course, said Father Larkin, —you've got the connection with Wittgenstein, and the song, what's it called, Van Morrison's song…

The young priest was nodding.

—You know the name of the song? said Father Larkin.

—Oh. I don't… I can't recall it, no.

—He's from your way, of course, Van Morrison. You're from Belfast, Father?

—I am indeed.

Father Larkin smiled at Stephen, then looked away and closed his eyes for a moment and held his hand in front of his face, his index finger pointing upwards.

—Streets of Arklow, said Father Larkin, and he opened his eyes.

—What's that now?

—The Van Morrison song. Obvious enough really. Tell me Father, do you know Father Dean Butler?

—Father Butler, I do indeed. Do you know Father Butler?

—We were at seminary together.

—You're a priest yourself?

The priest looked at Father Larkin sidelong, though he quickly composed himself.

—Yep, said Father Larkin. —I'm under cover as it were, on my holidays.

The priest nodded. He seemed almost frightened, and Stephen felt uncomfortable too. He wasn't sure what was going on, and he didn't like the statues in the church or the dry dusty smell of the incense.

—I know, I should probably keep the collar on at all times, in case of emergency, said Father Larkin. He seemed to be enjoying himself. —People might need baptising in the streets, you never know.

He laughed and the young priest smiled hesitantly, then shook his head. —Father Butler's no longer attached to this parish, he's away up Clones now, in Monaghan, he said.

—When did he transfer?

—Almost… I suppose it'd be a year ago. More. I believe he's happier there, he's settled in now, it's only a small parish. Do you mind me asking, where are you based, Father?

—Father Larkin. He held out his hand and they shook. —I'm here with a youth group, a football team. He gestured to Stephen. —Though if this one's as good at football as he is at snooker, we're looking at the new Diego Maradona.

The priest looked at Stephen and adjusted his glasses, which caught the sun and flashed.

—I was thinking, said Father Larkin, —that I'd love to get the boys in here to see the bells being rung. Or maybe they might even have a go? Would that be possible?

—How do you mean?

—Could we go up the bell tower and sit in while it rings? Or ring the bells ourselves. I think it could have a profound effect on the boys.

—I don't... How many boys?

—Sixteen, said Stephen.

—Sixteen, said Father Larkin.

—Oh, no. That's far too many. No, they'd never fit in there. Could you not drop by and stand in the grounds? It's a powerful sound from there, very beautiful. It'd catch anyone's heart.

—I might give Father Butler a shout about it, said Father Larkin.

—Father Butler's no longer attached to us, Father Larkin. He's away up in Clones now, he's not here.

Father Larkin nodded. —Not even in spirit, he said, and he guided Stephen and James along the aisle.

—My God, Dennis Taylor has joined the priesthood, Father Larkin said when they stepped outside, and Stephen remembered what Father Larkin had said when he first spoke to him in the school, that he knew what Stephen was thinking.

James Swann was sent home with Dillon on the train that evening. None of the lads, not even Stephen, knew what happened until they were gone an hour. Paddy Conroy would say no more, but Stephen pestered him.

—Stephen, it's out of my hands, James's ma and da can take care of it when he gets home, said Paddy, as he fried rashers in the big frying pan.

—Did James take the watch? asked Stephen.

—Well it was in his bag, so what do you think? Now look

Stephen, I'm after sayin' all I'm gonna say. James knows what's what, and it's up to his ma and da, it's nothin' to do with me now.

The rashers were spitting in the pan.

—James wouldn't rob that watch, said Stephen. He didn't believe that he would.

—Stephen, leave it, okay? Here, grab a few plates, help me with these. Paddy called over Fran Walsh as well. —Start butterin' up the bread, he said.

Fran peered into the pan. —What's the white stuff comin' off the rashers?

—Butter, now.

—Paddy, I don't think James took anything, James isn't a robber.

—Stephen, leave it.

Fran pointed at the pan. He said, —That's fat, that is.

It was like looking at space, Stephen thought. It was different every time, always changing. Stephen had first taken out the book on astronomy because the coloured dots that represented the stars and planets of the constellations made him think of the balls on the snooker table. He'd read some of the book, or tried to, but it was hard; he didn't understand some of the words.

Stephen was able to block out everything else when he looked at the snooker table and sized up a shot: he imagined where the balls would go, and where he'd leave the white for the next shot, how to keep things going. Each decision was connected to the next, like the dots on the space maps were connected. But on the table you could make a new constellation – constellation was a word he didn't know when he first picked the book, but he'd found out what it meant – every time you played. There was a constellation on the table and he was in control of it, although not totally in control; there was always something you didn't count on, always the balls and the baize and the cue and the cushions and your own body, something usually didn't do what you thought it would. But sometimes it was perfect and there was a thrill, a sense of control and of things falling into place, even if you knew it couldn't last. Though maybe you didn't want it to last. Maybe you needed to feel you were fighting against something, that you were in a scrap, a battle. Which you were, really, although mostly it was against yourself.

Stephen wouldn't sleep, he was sure. Paddy had lost it with him and told him to shut up about James and the watch. Then Stephen went to his room, where James's empty bed was.

It was very late now, but Father Larkin's car was still there, down below in the hostel yard. Stephen had watched the car pull in hours ago, and he'd watched the car as it sat there in the dark. Everyone was sleeping in the hostel now besides Stephen. He couldn't see anything inside the car, it was completely black, but he knew that it wasn't empty.

Stephen sat by the window, watching. He wondered what he would do. He wondered if he was able.

Harvest

Julian Gough

Judges' Comments

'Harvest' is a story in which very little happens—a woman
and her husband stay up late to watch the Oscars, and
have distracted conversations in which neither is quite
listening to the other, and, finally, make love. It's a sweet
and powerful evocation of a mature relationship, with the
suggestion of unfathomable loss at its heart. Oh; and the
world ends, terribly and awesomely and inescapably. And
whether you read the apocalypse as awesome prophecy or
tender metaphor, this is a superb story.

Author's Note

One morning, I decided I'd write a story, because I hadn't for a while. I sat down, and asked my subconscious, which is always composting experience into material, to give me something. The words 'I see the sun is alive' came into my head. I dutifully typed them. I had no idea what would happen next. I kept on writing, to find out. My subconscious kept coming up with more stuff. I was startled to discover how it all turned out. I wrote the ending, in longhand, lying on the floor, crying. Which doesn't happen often. And, many drafts later, it was done; but the core was solidly there from draft one (which is not always the case). Looked at objectively (which is definitely not how it was written), 'Harvest' is a mashup of 'Inconstant Moon' by Larry Niven and 'The Dead' by James Joyce: a loving critique of the exteriority (and thus shallowness of character) in American science fiction and of the interiority (and thus lack of action) in Irish realism. An attempt to use each to fix the other. And, of course, it's a story about love. I'm very happy with how it turned out. But I'm still not entirely sure who wrote it.

—*Julian Gough*

SHE WAS BRUSHING HER TEETH downstairs in the bathroom when he shouted from their bedroom, 'I see the sun is alive.'

She took out her toothbrush, and spat. Well, he can't be talking about their son. 'Whose son?' she said.

'Nobody's son,' came his voice down the stairs. 'The sun. The big yellah fellah in the sky. I see it's alive.'

She examined the spit as it slid down the curve of the sink. The spit paused, at the edge of the plughole. Pink spit. That wasn't good. Gum disease.

'It's what?' she said. 'What do you see?'

There had been a small bit of pink yesterday—just a streak in the white toothpaste—but now, all pink. Dark pink. Verging on red. Galloping gum disease.

'No,' he called down, 'I see in the paper.' She could hear him rattle the Weekend section of the *Irish Times* in her general direction.

'Who says?' she said. 'John Waters, no doubt. Don't mind him.'

'Scientists. Scientists say it. The sun is alive.'

'Oh, I heard something about that on the radio.' Should she floss? 'Was it Newstalk… it was.'

She would floss. She should have been flossing. The new dentist talked of little else. The man was obsessed with flossing. Last time she was in, to have the cap put back on, he had told her that the prisons in America had special, suicide-proof floss. Floss! It had never even occurred to her.

She pulled out a foot of floss, and, with a tug against the little bit of metal, cut it free.

'Leave the rifle out,' she called up. Last time he'd gone to Dublin, he'd left it in the gun cabinet, and taken the key with him. She hadn't slept well at all. Woke at every car that passed.

'Oh, I will yeah,' he called back.

She studied the floss, as she looped it around a finger. Gave a good tug, and the floss cut purple welts into the skin.

Well, it was certainly stronger than it looked. I suppose you could wrap it round your neck as easy. But it would never take the weight, surely. Still, I suppose, if you wove a few lengths of it together...

Three teeth in, she hit something solid.

She went after it cautiously with a finger. It wouldn't shift.

Tried again with the floss, and dislodged it.

A small, almost square bit of apple peel.

That was it. Irritating the gum. I should never have eaten that apple. Looked good. But, Lidl. Tasted of nothing.

Not gum disease.

She stood up straight. Gave herself a smile in the mirror. Not bad. Oh, she felt about twenty years younger. Must have been hanging over her since the first pink spit.

She gave her teeth a second, cheerful, brushing and went upstairs. She hadn't been enjoying the Oscars anyway. Up past her bedtime, and she didn't get any of the jokes. And the Cork girl hadn't won for make-up, so that was it for Ireland.

Glad enough when the set went on the blink, really.

In the bedroom, she took off her blouse.

'They're launching a probe at it,' he said, without looking up.

A divil for the paper. She slipped out of her skirt. The white edge of the Kindle or iPad or whatever it was they'd given him when he retired was just visible on the table beside the bed, sticking out from under a pile of books. Ah, he'd never go electronic.

'At what?' she said.

'The sun. They've discovered it's alive. That Solar Explorer yoke the yanks sent up.'

She studied her nightdress. State of it. 'Oh yes?' She'd get a new one.

'And now they're launching a little probe at it, at the sun. From the explorer.'

'Is that wise? If it's alive?' She took off her bra, found the jar—nearly out, better put it on the list—and rubbed a dab of moisturiser into the scar. Not bad at all. He'd done a great job, the little Indian fellow. Sure, it looked better than the real one. Ah, you'd get used to anything. Good to be alive.

'Well, they're doing it anyway,' he said. 'Tonight.'

He hopped up out of bed again—most unlike him—and went to the curtains.

Pulled them back.

'Oh that's right,' she said, hauling the nightdress on over her head. He's restless. All those young ones in their underwear at the Oscars, no doubt. 'Let the world get a good look at me.'

'Not a sinner up at this hour,' he said.

There were no houselights visible, out in the darkness. But the roofs of three or four houses across the fields, off the Thurles road, caught the moonlight coming through the clouds. Something odd about the light.

'Gangs down from Dublin,' she said. 'Looking for houses to rob.'

'Mmm. Could be.'

Was he listening to her at all? 'There was none of these gangs before the motorway,' she said.

'I suppose they couldn't get back home in time for their breakfast, before,' he said. Further off, the glow of Nenagh on the horizon didn't seem as bright as usual. No. That wasn't it. It was the clouds were too bright... 'Come here and look at this.'

The lid won't go back on the jar. 'Give me a minute,' she said.

Stuck. Start again... Ah, the smell is only lovely. Better than perfume. But sure, doesn't everything smell great these days.

She got the lid on, and came over. 'What?'

He said nothing.

The clouds were mad bright, and got even brighter as she crossed the room. It was more like twilight than the middle of the night.

And then the clouds parted, and they saw the moon.

'Holy shite,' he said.

'God, that's...' She wasn't sure if she was looking for a good word or a bad word. '... extraordinary.'

He looked away—the moon was nearly too bright to look at—and glanced at the fields.

It reminded him of the lighting in Old Trafford, the time he'd gone over with Philip. Bright, but not quite right. You could see every blade of grass, casting shadows that were too sharp... No, it's reminding him of something else, too...

'It's... beautiful,' she says beside him, but her voice is uncertain.

He remembers something he read, years back, in one of Philip's books. By... David Niven, no, that's the actor. Larry David... no, isn't he an actor as well? Or a comedian.

'Hang on,' he says. He's gone before she can bring herself to turn away from the moon.

He walks across the landing, and opens the door to Philip's old room.

Hesitates.

Jesus. State of the place.

She has racks of dresses and boxes of Christ knows what filling it, wall to wall. Christmas decorations. A couple of frying pans; in too bad a state to use, but too good to throw out. Piles of neatly folded, pale green curtains that the assistant manager had given her in lieu of wages, when they'd closed the hotel. He edges around and through the stuff till he gets to Philip's old bed.

He kneels on it, and his knees sink deep into the soft mattress as he leans forward to look at the bookshelves.

Philip's books.

He remembers the year he'd read his way through the lot of them, like he was looking for clues. Old paperbacks, mostly. Second hand. Cheap.

He pulls one out at random, flips it open. A yellow, brittle, paper smell. Cool, dusty; like an attic. The pencilled price inside the front cover, £1.20. That'd be from Mick Tunny's place on Sarsfield Street. Got with the pocket money, before the euro came in.

As he kneels there, the book vibrates in his hands, as the muscles across his shoulders clench and unclench. His body knows something is up, it wants him to do something; but he's not ready yet, and besides, it's probably nothing. A bright moon. It's nothing.

He pulls out another, opens it.

Big, square, black, ink stamp, *Liberty Books, Limerick*, and the price neatly handwritten below in blue biro. Two quid. Ah yeah. That place with no windows that also did car number plates, and smelt of paint. No light, no ventilation, ridiculous.

Kids used to get high on that stuff. The aerosols.

He sniffs the trembling book. Nothing.

We'd drop off Philip, she'd do a full day's shopping, and on the way back to the carpark I'd nip in to pick him up. No matter how long we'd left him, he was never ready to leave. The only noise in the place the rattle of the little ball, as the owner shook the can.

Bald fellah. Just sitting behind the counter, working away. Oh, and then the little hiss, as he sprayed the stencil. Never anyone else there. Long gone, now.

He puts the book back carefully.

He glances along the shelves.

A lot of the Penguins with the black spines from Charlie Byrne's in Galway. The university years. Hard chewing. A few of those had defeated him.

Oh, the different eras. And then the few years towards the end, when he had the job for a while, and he was able to afford books new. Eason's. Dubray.

Outside, as the birds are woken by the strange light, there are the beginnings of a confused dawn chorus.

His throat is very dry. He clears it. All right.

Which one was it? He reads a few titles off the top shelf. History, no. He moves along, down to the next shelf, thrillers. Reads a few more titles, science fiction, yes, these are all the science fiction. In alphabetical order. Which doesn't help, because he still can't remember who wrote it. Ah Philip, your shoes never tied, and the arse of your trousers hanging around the backs of your knees, and your homework always a disgrace if you did it at all, you little fucker; but you always had such neat bookshelves.

He pulls one out to have a look at the cover. It was green, looked like a jigsaw, he'll know it when he sees it.

No. Not that one.

Pulls out another with a greenish spine. But the cover itself isn't green.

Another. No.

Then there is an inexplicable rush of energy through him, it's like he's grabbed an electric fence. He hauls an armful of books off the shelf, and flings them across the bed. Half of them keep going and end up on the floor, and he gives out a big sob like a cough.

He goes on all fours on the bed, and closes his eyes, and lowers his head for a minute.

When he opens his eyes, it's right there on the bed in front of him. Larry Niven. That's the one. *All The Myriad Ways*. Myriad? No wonder he hadn't remembered it.

He gets off the bed, and flips the book open at the list of contents; that was it, 'Inconstant Moon.' He turns to the story and, standing there, starts reading. It takes a while to get going, so he skips. Reads. Skips. Reads.

Yes. This is it.

After a few pages, he walks—runs nearly—back to their bedroom with the book.

'The sun,' he says, coming in the door. 'It's gone nova.'

'Nova?' She has trouble placing the word, it's not a word she expects to hear from his mouth. Novena, Nova Scotia, November, Vauxhall Nova—Matty O'Connor used to drive one till he won the Lotto and moved to Thailand—wasn't there a joke about the Vauxhall Nova, yes, not a joke; nobody in Spain would buy them, because Nova was the Spanish for Doesn't Go...

'It's exploded.' He points up at the blazing moon. It's throwing light as bright as dawn in through the window now.

'The moon's exploded?' she says.

'The sun, the sun's exploded, it's exploding. That's its light, bouncing off the moon. It must be melting the rocks up there.'

Ag scoilteadh na gcloch, she thinks. She'd learned it for her Leaving Cert. Oh, all the stock phrases. *Bhí na néalta boga bána ag snámh go leisciúil trasna na spéire*. Got a B. 'You've lost me, go back,' she says. He's in a funny mood tonight. 'What's a nova?'

'A star, like the sun, the sun is a star...'

'I know that...'

'... exploding,' he says.

She tries to make the connection with their lives, with this room.

'The sun,' she says. 'Exploding.' Is he serious? She glances up, at the crazy moon, and back at him.

Ah, he's making a hames of this. 'Anyway,' he says, brusquely. 'That's the light and the heat of it, bouncing off the moon.'

'But... why?'

'I don't know,' he says.

'God, maybe the sun really is alive,' she says. 'Maybe we shouldn't have poked it with that probe. Do you think it's coming to have a good look at us, because we went and had a look at it?'

Is she mocking him?

'How the fuck should I know?' he says, and she realises that he is serious, that this is serious, and she goes quiet. 'Sorry...' he says.

'I was just wondering, why now,' she says, not looking at him. Looking at the moon. Yes, it looks all wrong. All the detail's gone. There's just a glare, like a headlight.

'Look,' he says, 'stars, they all...' He can't bring himself to say *explode*, '... go nova, eventually, for some reason.' Back on firmer ground now. 'Melt their moons and their planets and their, I don't know, comets, it's normal...'

'Normal!'

'Ah you know what I mean.'

'But is it doing this *deliberately*?' she says, and now she really is trying to understand. 'Is it anything to do with us at all? Did we... did we annoy it, or wake it...'

His foot taps the carpet. Oh God, let's wrap this up. He needs to do something.

'Or did we set it off,' she says, 'like a...'

'You're trying to find an answer, there isn't an answer,' he says. 'Lookit, the sun's, what, thousands of times bigger than the earth...'

'More, probably.'

'So you're not going to work it out. It's...' He pauses. What is it? 'Mysterious. Like God used to be.'

He closes his eyes, to think. They need to understand, all right. But not the why of it. Christ knows why. The what of it. What will happen next. No point just running around like eejits.

'But,' she says, and pauses. But what? 'But we'll be grand. Won't we?'

He wants to say yes. But he doesn't say yes. He just opens his eyes.

The look on his face. Oh dear God.

'No,' he says. 'It's not just happening to the moon. It must be melting the rocks, and more than the rocks, round the other side of the world already. The day side.'

She's trying to remember her science classes, but the teacher was useless, Sister Imelda, poor woman, she ended up in Thurles, on a locked ward.

The sun, the sun…

It's too long ago. 'Wait…' she says, and she tries to remember instead the episodes of *Doctor Who* and *Star Trek* and God knows what that Philip used to try and make her watch. The earth was always being destroyed in those. Yes. 'But it's only eight minutes,' she says, 'isn't it, for the light to reach us. From the sun. So if anything bad was to happen… it's already happened.'

'It's not the light we have to worry about,' he says. 'The other stuff, the, what do you call it, the plasma, the gas, hasn't even arrived yet. And it's, what, I don't know, millions of degrees.' He's explaining it to himself as he explains it to her; trying to imagine it, to see it in his head. 'We have the whole earth between us and the sun now. Because it's the night. But…'

He closes his eyes again, to see it better, to work it out. 'The heat of the sun will boil the oceans…'

He's like a man having a vision, she thinks, as she listens to the extraordinary words coming out of him. A prophet. She studies his face, astonished.

When he's explained, it, when it's sunk in—no it hasn't sunk in, but when it starts to begin the long process of sinking in—'How long?' she says.

'I don't know. I'll have a look at the book. I think he says...' He pulls open the book so hard that the glue in the binding, stiff and yellow with age, gives way, and the spine cracks in two with a sound like a rifle shot. Each sees, in the corner of their vision, the other's face tighten.

'What's the book?' she says.

'One of Philip's.' He doesn't look up. 'It has a story in it about this class of a thing, novas, flares, the sun. All the details. Whisht a minute...'

He's scrambling back through the story again. Skipping the bits where the man and the woman go shopping, go to a bar, talk shite in the bright moonlight. Skip, skip, skip... here we go. Yes. The story has it all worked out... But, sure, it's only a book, it's science fiction—entertainment—how can you tell if he isn't making half of it up, the science?

'Dawn,' she says, thinking it through. 'We're spinning towards it.'

Oh God, now I've convinced her; but what if I'm wrong? Declaring the end of the world over a harvest moon? He keeps his head down in the book.

'We can't avoid it,' she says, 'Dawn...' and he can can hear the first little stir of fear in her voice.

Sweat breaks out high on his forehead, just at the hairline, and he doesn't know if it's embarrassment or terror. He wipes it away surreptitiously, and reads on.

But it's so convincing. It describes it exactly. And as he thinks that, the light outside the window lurches brighter.

'No,' he says, looking up from the broken book, suddenly certain. 'The atmosphere is already on fire, around there in the daylight. Everything's on fire.'

'Oxygen,' she says, uncertainly.

He shrugs, nods. 'It's all expanding and exploding, everything. The oceans are boiling, they're coming around the curve of the world towards us. In both directions. All directions. It'll be here long before dawn.'

But now it's her gets the doubt, he can see it rise in her, and it brings his own doubt back, and he is simultaneously both certain he is right, and sure he must be, somehow, wrong. He glances at the window, the hot, white moonlight burning through the glowing clouds.

An old cowboy song comes into his head. He used to sing it to Philip, when Philip would come out to the shed to watch him working a bit of wood. Ah Philip. The fingers would go into the ears, the minute the angle grinder came on, or the sander. But if you sang over the noise, Philip would take the fingers out, and sing along.

Ghost riders in the sky...

The galvanised roof of the shed gave it a nice reverb.

'Come on, we'll go find out,' he says, 'One way or the other.'

They go downstairs, to see is the news covering it, but they can't find the remote for the TV, just the one for the box.

And it's this—not being able to find the remote—that sets her heart, at last, pumping faster, so that her breathing grows rapid, then ragged, as she searches.

She finds it—she'd left it in her chair, and it had slid down behind the cushion—and hauls it out. Goes to hand it to him, apologetic, but he just nods at the dead screen. She steadies herself—three deep breaths—and turns on the television. Braced for anything.

A vision of the apocalypse.

The inferno.

But the screen just goes straight from black to a harsh, bright blue. White words appear.

No signal.

Wait... 'Is the box on?' she says.

He looks.

It is.

'Of course, it's a satellite job,' he says.

Satellite TV.

Satellites.

He's never thought of them as real before, as actual objects, metal and plastic, put together by men like him, but of course they must be. He's never seen them, but they must exist. He sees them now, in his mind for a second, whirling through the cold and dark. The nothingness.

He shakes the vision out of his head. 'They must have all gone up like midges in a gorse fire,' he says.

She tries to remember what she actually saw, when the Oscars went on the blink; was there a flash? Had she actually seen the end of the world? But no, it had just stopped. One minute someone she'd never heard of was making a joke about something she didn't understand; next minute, a blue screen...

'The radio,' she says.

The radio—sturdy, old, pre-digital—sits on the counter, tucked in behind the toaster. Nearly as big as it.

She flicks it on, and tries to find a channel. The radio just roars at them, no sign of a station, until she gets to 103 on the dial.

Tipp FM. It must be the only one close enough to pick up through the static, sure they can see the transmitter out the kitchen window, up on Keeper Hill.

Conor Lally is reading out the death notices, and for a moment they are reassured by the normality of it. Ordinary, quiet, local deaths.

'*The following deaths have occurred... Edmond (Ned) Maguire, Kilburry, Cloneen. Reposing in Brett's Funeral Home, Mullinahone, from five o'clock on Monday evening with removal at seven thirty to the Church of the Nativity, Cloneen. Funeral Mass on Tuesday at eleven, followed by burial in the adjoining cemetery...*'

In ancient reflex, they shush and listen.

'*...Brother Martin Looby, Mount Saint Joseph Abbey, Roscrea. Reposing in Mount Saint Joseph Abbey Church from 10am on Monday. Funeral Mass on Tuesday at 11 o'clock, followed by burial immediately afterwards in the Monastic Cemetery...*'

Next one up is some auld wan from Ardcrony. Next up, a Hackett from Goold's Cross.

'Well, we haven't made the death notices, so we must be alive,' he says. Ah, he's beginning to hope. Even Tipp FM would have to interrupt their schedules for the end of the world.

But since when was Conor up at this hour, she thinks? He'd be home in bed hours ago, after a couple of pints in Rocky's.

'It's a recording,' she says. 'For America. There's no one there.'

'Ah shite,' he says.

'*Sadie O'Meara, Corville Road, Roscrea and formerly of Cloughjordan, reposing at her residence on Monday from two o'clock with rosary at eight. Private removal on Tuesday morning...*'

She switches it off. They give each other a look. They are getting a bit giddy now.

'The internet,' he says.

She digs her old, cracked tablet out of her handbag on the counter top, and turns it on. She hasn't used it for a couple of days, but the screen brightens anyway. There's still a bit of charge, good. Then there's an animated swirl of light, like a galaxy revolving, that turns into the word SAMSUNG. A long pause; the two of them stare at their dim reflections in the glass of the dark, cracked screen.

This is like my treasure hunt, she thinks. My heart going wild, searching everywhere for something, and I'm not even sure what.

She only ever had the one birthday party—a foreign idea at the time, God knows where her mother even got the notion—and it was such a disaster her mother never tried again. Broken presents, children crying, and a Cahalan fell into the slurry pit.

But she had enjoyed the treasure hunt her father had organised, around the yard, and the outhouses, and finally back into the good room... No one had known he'd had that in him, the creativity. The little maps!

. She closes her eyes, and sees her father's face, so embarrassed (and proud maybe? yes), when she had thanked him. And him dead within the year. And they didn't let her go, they didn't let her go to the funeral.

But at least she got the one thing right. Because, seeing his surprise when she thanked him, she'd had the sudden fear: he doesn't know I love him.

It was like coughing up a stone, saying it, her throat tightening up, it came out sore and thin, sure nobody said that kind of thing. But she had said it, in time. That was the best thing she'd ever done. He'd known.

She has screwed her eyes so tightly closed, she's getting pains now in the muscles under them.

She opens them, and she's staring at a screen. Oh yes. The Samsung. Her reflection. His.

The dark screen lights up, and they vanish.

It connects; there's still an internet, and for a moment their hopes rise, as though that means everything is fine, will be fine.

'Find a news site,' he says, like he knows what he's talking about. Peering down at it like a man looking down a well, trying to spot a body.

News. The BBC. They have the resources. They'll know.

The BBC site tells her to try again in a minute. She tries again in a minute.

Nothing.

RTÉ's website just says '404 Error'.

CNN...

No.

Sky News...

No.

She googles 'News Sites', and after an agonisingly long pause gets a list of answers. She starts clicking her way down the list.

No.

No.

No.

She finally gets a jittery newscaster from Italy or Spain maybe: he's trying to seem calm. Failing.

They stare at his perspiring, jabbering face; lean in over him till their heads touch.

'I can't understand a word he's saying,' she says after a minute, heart pounding, and goes on to the next site.

It won't load.

The next starts loading, then freezes.

They've searched every news site on the first page of the search results.

He's looking at her. He always leaves it to her, the computer stuff.

Normally she'd ring Jim Hickey at this stage. Jim set up the Samsung for her when she got it; she knows there's probably a better way of doing this. Jim used to service the computers for the Council, till they amalgamated Tipperary North Riding with Tipp South Riding, and let Jim go. But no, she couldn't ring him at this hour.

She tries to go back to the Italian fellow, but now that site won't load either. She stares at the screen. Surely they could find out what's happening… search for… who, NASA? Sure, aren't they all in America? They'd all be dead already.

Other scientists?

Experts?

Where?

How?

'I don't know where to begin,' she says, and her eyes prickle, and she rubs them. 'I'm sorry.'

'It wouldn't make any difference,' he says, and puts an arm around her shoulder.

They shut down the Samsung; switch off the box, the television, the radio, at the wall; as though they are saving electricity; as though they are trying to protect the house from fire.

They stand in the silent room. Birdsong, outside.

Surely there must be something else they can do, he thinks. But nothing comes to him.

'I need to go to the bathroom,' she says.

'Off you go,' he says.

She closes the bathroom door behind her, very quietly. As though she doesn't want him to know she's closing the door on him. Doesn't want him to feel alone.

As she sits on the toilet, she thinks, the world is ending.

What an idea.

Not just me. The world.

Everyone in it.

Everything.

No, she can say it; she can think it; but she can't feel it, yet.

She's assuming he's still going to Dublin. He always goes to Dublin, weekends. And wouldn't he want to go more than ever, tonight, if there's time? He can't wait till morning…

But she doesn't want him to go. She hasn't gone herself for nearly two years.

A line from the Book of Revelation comes to her.

'Go and pour out on the earth the seven bowls of the wrath of God.'

Sarah Duggan used to say that, pretending to be Father Keating. What was her next line, deadly serious face on her... 'Porridge', that was it. 'Cornflakes. Rice Krispies. Soup...'

She hasn't read the bible since leaving school. Mind you, she'd read a fierce amount of it then. Oh, mother of Jesus, Christian Doctrine, with Sister Stan, back from the missions.

Funny; back then, Sister Stanislaus forgetting your name—forgetting everybody's name, forgetting what she'd just said—it was considered perfectly normal behaviour for an auld wan.

No doctor required. No diagnosis.

Sure, wasn't she just getting a bit shook, no problem, put her in charge of a class of bored teenagers. Jesus, the poor woman.

Must get more prunes. Lidl has the jars on offer.

That was a mad class. Sister Stan would leave you alone if you looked like you were reading the bible, so they'd all be reading Revelations, for the horror. Or the Song of Solomon, for the sex... definitely a woman wrote that, definitely.

There we go.

She wipes. A little sore round the back. This paper's very harsh. Aldi. We should have put in a bidet, when he got the retirement money.

She pauses, about to wipe again.

Arra, yes.

She pulls off the nightdress instead, and hops into the shower.

A quick wash. Why not. May as well die clean.

Stand out of the way till the water warms up.

Revelations. Now, that's all about the end of the world. *'His eyes were like a flame of fire,'* she'd always laughed at that one, 'What are you laughing at, child?' 'I'm laughing with joy because God loves me, Sister.' 'Oh. Very good.' Suspicion in the cracked auld voice, but what could Sister Stan say to that? Of course it was a flame of fire, what other kind was there? A flame of water? A flame of dirt?

She gets the water right. A little warmer, maybe. Why not. Lovely...

Water... *'His voice was like the roar of many waters...'*

John Waters! What would he make of the end of the world? That'd be a good column. He'd be pleased, no doubt. Something to get his teeth into.

More lines from Revelations are coming back to her. She'd had no idea they were all still in there.

'Behold, he is coming with the clouds, and every eye will see him...'

Blinking in the warm water, the steamy air of the shower, she sees the boiling oceans, roaring around the world, in a wall of superheated steam and fire....

'And his face was like the sun shining in full strength...'

Jesus, maybe it was all true.

'...But fire came down from heaven and consumed them.'

There you go. Fire came down from heaven and consumed them.

She turns it up a fraction. Hotter. No point saving the oil.

Oh, beautiful.

Sister Stan, Sister Stan... she'd had to take sports—camogie— the one time, when flu had decimated the staff. That was beyond chaos. That had been frightening. The Farrell twins from St Joseph's Park, settling a few scores. The parents were alcoholics, God love them, the same clothes every day, and the smell off them, oh now you'd feel for them, you'd call the Social Services, but then... Jesus, they were just terrifying. The glee in their eyes.

A few of the others joined in, ganging up on the unpopular girls. They'd skelped Sinead Tracy off the pitch. The father a solicitor, of course. She'd run off to the dressing rooms bleeding from a cut behind her ear, and crying.

The girls had gone so far, they'd lost their nerve, they nearly wanted a real teacher to come onto the pitch, and take over and calm it all down.

And, after, she remembered the way Sister Stanislaus had looked at her, at her face, at her... yes, as she stepped out of the shower. Just a look. Only a look.

Sister Stan had loved her. Holy God. That was it. The poor woman. Had she ever been kissed. Oh, the poor woman.

As she dries herself she thinks, and now those hairs are grey. Grey! Extraordinary.

She gives the area a closer look. A bit scraggly. Could do with a trim. Nothing drastic, now, but a few clips with the nail scissors... She pulls out the little pedal bin and, standing slightly awkwardly astride it, with one foot on the pedal to keep the lid open, trims the triangle of grey hair. Pushes the bin away in under the sink. Pulls on her nightdress again.

He'd still have time to drive to Dublin to see Philip... but the hospital won't be open. He could wake them up, but no they'll be awake, surely, with all this carry on... Ah sure don't they have a night shift, night nurses, what's he thinking.

And what would he do? Sit beside Philip, and say what? That they love him, that they always loved him, that they always will love him; that they are sorry, even if they don't know what it is they should be sorry for? Again? Say it again?

A merciful release. For all of them.

She comes out of the bathroom at last.

'I'm not going to Dublin,' he says.

She nods. As a child, she had believed in the resurrection of the body. But a few years of sitting beside Philip's body, watching her son grow old without recognising her voice... No, she doesn't believe in the resurrection of the body any more.

Oh, she'd thought at the time she should blame the rifle, hate the rifle.

But it wasn't the rifle.

She's often held the rifle since, when himself's away visiting Philip. Sat up in bed herself, holding it, and wondered what Philip had been thinking, just before he pulled the trigger. Why he didn't walk across the landing, and come in, and talk to them. She wanted to go upstairs now, and walk across the landing, and walk ten, twelve, fourteen, sixteen years back in time; and go in and say they didn't mind about the money, they didn't mind about the house, what family hadn't got burned on property?

No, it wasn't the rifle. She's grown fond of it; old, simple, and well made. Wood and steel, no more immoral than a shovel. Protecting her from harm, as if to make up for what Philip had made it do. The wood glowed under the varnish. The cool steel gleamed under the oil. He still kept it perfectly. It had hunted the rabbits that had paid for his tickets to the dance where they'd met. So long ago. How fast Ireland had changed.

She realises he is looking at her, that they have just been standing at the foot of the stairs looking at each other.

'Will we go to bed,' he says. It sets off echoes of all the other times he's said that over the years.

'Yes,' she says.

He pats her on the bottom, as she walks up the stairs ahead of him.

In bed, it's nearly like they're shy at first. Out of the habit. Which they are not, particularly. But the odd shyness doesn't last long.

As he's doing all the hard work of warming her up, she thinks, this is great. And, a thought that she's often had in these moments;

Harvest

why don't the young people just do this all the time?

Why don't we?

Oh, to think we didn't do this for years, what a waste.

He comes up from down below, to join her.

She reaches, reflexively, for the K-Y Jelly in the bedside drawer.

No. She lets her hand relax, fall back on the pillow. No need, they're both well ready for it tonight.

There.

Oh God, that's lovely.

Through decades of habit—no, more accurate to say practice, experience—they adjust to each other's rhythm; like old jazz musicians improvising on a standard.

They have no idea how good they are at this now, after so many decades, but they are as good as it gets.

*

'*Then I saw a new heaven and a new earth, for the first heaven and the first earth had passed away, and the sea was no more.*'

Around the curve of the world, it sweeps towards Ireland, taking the Atlantic with it. The wave's approach crackles the sky; it is as though a thousand suns are rising in the West; rising incredibly fast; and then it arrives, and it is indeed the sun, descended to earth like a God: transforming, transcending, turning everything to light. It evaporates the water out of Galway Bay, like God stooping to drink, and sweeps—miles high, tens of miles, hundreds—across the cold, black Cliffs of Moher till they glow red, then white. Then melt. Then evaporate.

'*The fourth angel poured out his bowl on the sun and it was allowed to scorch people with fire.*'

The golden plasma sweeps inland, through Donegal and Sligo,

Mayo and Galway, Clare and Kerry.

It lifts the Shannon from its bed of rock and turns its dark cold waters to light and plasma, and sweeps on, towards the unfinished house by Lough Derg that Philip never lived in, its bare concrete rooms long ago pissed in and shat in by teenage bush drinkers, grown now with jobs, or emigrated. The house on whose exposed roof beams their only begotten son had been crucified.

'And the fire came down from heaven, and consumed the burnt offering and the sacrifices; and the glory of the lord filled the house.'

The golden plasma rolls across the dark central plain, faster than the sound of its own approach, throwing only its light ahead of itself. The woken birds, the confused and uneasy night animals, turn to face the hot, hard light, but only for a moment, before a wave ten, then fifty, then a hundred miles high arrives over the low Tipperary hills that were once the highest mountains in Europe, three hundred million years ago. The trees flare brilliant an instant and birds, animals, trees, are gone.

'So he who sat on the cloud swung his sickle across the earth, and the earth was reaped.'

And the golden wave rolls on across the moon-bright pastures and the dozing cattle. Through the Golden Vale. Across the Rock of Cashel on which they would never now be buried, blasting the names of parents and grandparents from their tall stone cross, igniting the quartz.

Melting the iron spears around her father's grave so fast they don't have time to fold and puddle but just evaporate to iron gas, then ions, then plasma too, joining the great wave.

The thorns of the blackthorn bushes on the far slopes of the Rock hold their shape for an instant in light and are gone, even their ash incandescent and joining the wave of light flooding across Ireland, the descent of their last end.

And now the other wave of light comes around the Eastern curve of the world; across Asia; across Europe; it reaches Dublin, taking Philip back to where he came from, taking everyone home. Every atom, born in a sun, returns, as the two great waves of energy encircle the dark earth, like arms around a sleeping child. Across Kildare, Laois, Offaly it comes; across Tipperary, transforming the houses of their neighbours into light. The sun reaches out to the earth, and embraces it.

'They will need no light of lamp or sun, for the Lord God will be their light, and they will reign forever and ever.'

For an instant, before the two waves meet above them, they are the last two people on earth. Adjusting their timing, each totally aware of the pleasure of the other, their souls swoon; and in this moment they know each other's essence so totally that they have forgotten each other's names, as animal and human join, humanity and god, matter and spirit, and all become one; they become incandescent; and all the particles that made their patterns leap to higher levels; and the energies of the last woman and the last man join, and change form, and transcend form, as at the last instant she thinks; what else is there but love; as he thinks; what the fuck else is there, but love?

The Iron Age

Arja Kajermo

Judges' Comments

The Iron Age' is set in post-war Finland when the country is dominated by the Soviet Union and forgotten by the rest of the world. Seen through a young narrator's eyes, life is full of hardships and puzzlement and dark humours. A memorable chronicle of a family's struggle during a less well-known period in history.

Author's Note

The advice to writers is usually 'write about what you know'. This is what I have done in 'The Iron Age'.

I wanted to give a sense of how war casts a long shadow and how children internalise their parents' wars. I started writing the story with a plan to turn it into a graphic novel but I found that the words took over in the telling. Before I knew it, I had the story told better in words than I would have in pictures.

Also I found it liberating to tell this story in English (not my first language) because it put the subject at a bit of a remove which made it easier to tell. I was on a roll writing it.

—*Arja Kajermo*

IT WAS FINLAND, it was the nineteen-fifties but on our farm it could have been the Iron Age. We had a horse to take us places, the dirt track allowed no cars near us. I was four and had never seen a car but I had seen a picture of one. We had heard of electricity but we didn't have it. Time moved slowly then and things did not change much. The winters were colder and the summers were hotter.

One such hot day Grandmother took me with her to visit her niece Miina. My hair was plaited tight till it hurt. My eyes were pulled into slits. If I had dared I would have sobbed. The boots hurt too. They were hand-me-downs from my older brother, made for him by Mother's father who was a shoemaker.

Grandmother moved uphill along the dirt road at a steady pace like a Russian tank. It was hard to keep up.

The dirt road was only wide enough for a horse and cart but the trees around it had been cut down to the width of a boulevard in Helsinki. Miina's husband Aleksis had cut the fir trees down when Miina had started crying shortly after their wedding. She had cried for weeks until people started talking. Word got around. When word gets around, help is on the way. That was the way it was in our parish.

Married men came to give advice to Aleksis. They told him what all married men knew. Women get depressed if the pine trees grow too close to the house. Pine trees are dark trees and their

ominous rustling brings on sadness in women. Aleksis cleared an
area the size of several fields around the house. Still Miina cried.
She wouldn't stop.

The married men came back. It was true that Aleksis had cut a
lot of trees and the timber would pay for a whole season's fertiliser,
which was good. But he would have to do better, for women can
be hard to please. Cut more, said the men, come on now, give her
a view.

So Aleksis cut a wide path along the dirt road so that Miina
could see all the way to Grandmother's farm from her kitchen
window. She stopped crying then. And Aleksis bought fertiliser for
the money he got for the timber. And also a few metres of nice blue
fabric with a flower pattern for a new dress and a few metres of
chequered cotton for a new pinafore for Miina. Quite a few metres
because Miina had got quite stout from lying in bed crying.

Miina enjoyed visitors. She clapped her hands with pleasure
when people entered her house. And we had brought her a cake
made with five big hen eggs.

Eggs were hard to come by for we had no hens. We had rowed
across the lake to the rich relations and mentioned our lack of eggs
and the farmer had offered us a good laying hen. Just take one, he
said. So Grandmother had taken me outside and pointed at a hen
and said catch that one. And I had spent the afternoon chasing the
hen until we were both exhausted and Grandmother was in a rage.
A boy had to be got to catch the hen and put it in a sack for us.

We rowed home all pleased but the hen would not lay. The
blasted creature seemed to change its nature. It grew a cock's comb
and spurs and became vicious. We had to chase it away into the
forest for the fox to eat.

'I would not eat a dirty bird like that,' Grandmother said, 'they
feed from the dung heap.'

So we rowed to the other end of the lake and told the other rich relatives about the bad hen we had been given and how we had no eggs. And they had sent a child to find eggs for us. Really good eggs they were and we returned to thank them when they were all gone. We never rowed home without our half dozen eggs.

'To be the poor relation of rich people is good in some ways and bad in other ways,' said Grandmother, pulling hard at the oars.

Now five of those eggs had gone into the cake that Grandmother had baked for Miina. We stepped quietly into the house because we had manners. People from the town bang on doors and shout greetings when entering, startling people who may be having a midday nap.

And indeed Miina seemed to be napping in her rocking chair when we entered but when she became aware of us her big face lit up and she clapped her hands.

Grandmother made the usual formal apology: 'Here we are, God help us, disturbing good hardworking people…'

'So you are!' said Miina with feeling. And then her chin fell towards her bosom and her eyes closed. The rocking chair continued to rock. A light snoring buzz surrounded the scene.

Miina had fallen asleep.

It was a habit Miina had. She fell asleep at odd times. She had fallen asleep when she was getting married and had to be shaken and shouted at to be woken for the 'I do'. She fell asleep in the sauna. She fell asleep making hay. She fell asleep milking. And she fell asleep when visitors came.

Grandmother and I looked at each other. Had Miina really told us so rudely that we were unwelcome? Surely not. We watched while Miina slept and listened to the sound of bluebottles and Miina's snoring. Time seemed to stand still.

In the end we stood up to leave. Grandmother hesitated but then she took the cake.

It would have been wrong to leave Miina a reminder of our visit and her embarrassing lapse.

We walked back down the hill all subdued and full of thoughts. Grandmother sighed heavily and muttered to herself. She said that Miina should keep her eyes open more. Aleksis had been wandering, she said, he had been seen with a married woman behind a barn and more than once too. There had been tracks in the snow and in the muck. His boots and smaller boots. He had been seen where he should not have been seen. And sometimes it was hard to blame him—what with Miina letting herself go like that.

Not that Aleksis would get away with anything, the little scut! Next time he was seen at dusk stern measures would be taken.

He would do well to consider what had happened to his dog Nalle who had turned out bad and had to be shot in the end which was a shame for such a promising dog.

But that is another story.

2

Let me tell you the story of Nalle and Nille. They were both fine dogs of a breed called Finnish Spitz. They are hunting dogs and very economical in their whelping. There are usually no more than four in a litter.

When four pups were born to the good hunting bitch at Moor House Farm the pups were carefully placed with the relations. The strongest was earmarked for Miina who was a daughter of the farm. Or Miina's Aleksis rather, for what use is a dog to a woman? The second and third were also promising looking and went to a strong farmer nearby. Father got the fourth. Father's great uncle pushed the pup forward with the toe of his boot.

'That one is for you,' he said.

Aleksis's pup looked like a bear so it was given a bear's name—

Nalle. Ours was named Nille because it rhymes with Nalle. It was a name with no meaning but it is good to rhyme names. There is comfort and continuity in rhyming. Nalle-Nille-Kille-Kalle. Or Marja-Tarja-Arja-Irja. Endless possibilities.

Father was a bit miffed about getting the runt. But he was glad to have a dog because he was a keen hunter and a good shot. When his grey eyes fastened on a bird his rifle would go to his shoulder and the bird would drop from the sky. He seldom missed because he had practised on Russians for four years at the front.

But Aleksis was a few years younger and had not been in the war. He could not hit a bottle on a tree stump, damn it. It was unfair that he should have Nalle, the better dog.

Anyway, Nille was coming on. She was a natural. She did not need telling, she knew what to do. She turned her grey puppy coat into the red adult coat of the spitz. Her tail curled over her back, her ears were pricked, she looked alert.

Apart from the legs being on the short side she looked unusually pure bred for a village dog. She was the real thing. The pitch-black nose twitched, she was ready to go.

And when she ran into the forest it was not long before machine gun bursts of barking were heard. Ra-ra-ra-rah! Ra-ra–ra-rah-rah-rah! She had found a capercaillie and she had chased it up a tree. The bird sat high up in the tree watching the barking dog. Nille's tail spun like a propeller, making the bird dizzy. Nille knew to bark from the other side of the tree so that when Father caught up he could take aim and shoot the bird in the back.

And Father carried the large bird home and threw it proudly on the floor for Mother to deal with. It is said of the capercaillie that it tastes of turpentine because of its diet of pine cones. But we had a diet of potatoes and gruel and pine-cone-flavoured meat was a welcome change.

Mother set to without delay and by the evening we had a huge stew. Such happiness! And what pride we took in our fine loyal hound Nille.

Nalle on the other hand...

Nalle did not live up to expectations. To begin with his coat did not turn the right red colour. He had black marks along the sides. One of his ears hung at a jaunty angle instead of being pricked up like the ears of a Finnish Spitz should be.

There was something of the hare-hound about him, the men said. Would he be good for hunting hares or would he go for the capercaillie, they mused.

It turned out he was good for neither.

Nalle was pursuing his own agenda. He kept running away. Like all dogs he spent most of the day chained in the yard to keep watch. But the minute he was released he disappeared into the undergrowth and was gone for days. When he was brought home on a chain he was sullen and uncooperative.

During one runaway episode he was seen chasing ewes. This meant Nalle was for the bullet. Aleksis had to put his rifle into Nalle's ear and pull the trigger.

'A distance from which it is hard to miss,' the men muttered. And took deep pulls on their cigarettes and coughed.

After this we were extra pleased with our Nille. The runt had turned into one of Father's triumphs.

And there were not many of them.

3

'Eleven years ago on this day Risto was fatally wounded...'

Every morning Mother and Father got up at four if it was summer and five if it was winter. If I woke I would stay in bed and listen to their quite murmuring as they spoke companionably over breakfast in the kitchen. Every day was an anniversary of someone's death. Some had died in their beds from a fever or a weak heart or old age, but most had fallen in the war. They never mentioned birthdays. After all a child has achieved nothing except being born and any fool could do that. A Godmother would send their Godchild a card when the child's name-day came up in the calendar. But a birthday? Better wait and see if you amounted to anything by the time you died; whether you were worth mentioning at all or best forgotten.

Then Mother and Father would discuss what they had dreamt in the night. There were secret clues in these dreams and omens for the future. Or warnings about people who seemed like your friends but were secretly ill-disposed to you. Sometimes the dead came back with messages. The meaning of a dream was a riddle that could be hard to tease out.

'He was coming up from the lake and stopped by the rowan tree and gave me a strange smile... Then he turned back without saying anything ... What do you think it means?'

'A smile is a good thing?' Mother was always looking for good signs. But Father was cautious and slow to be reassured.

'It was more of a sarcastic smile.'

Then it was time for them to go out and see to the cattle and Mother had to get the cows milked. I went back to sleep.

When they came back in for their 'second breakfast' the day started for real and things got tense. Father barked orders.

'Up! Out! And about!'

That meant Tapio and Tuomas, who were seven and eight, had to get up, get ready and start walking the five kilometres to school.

It was a long walk for small boys with short legs. Sometimes Father's uncle on the next farm would give them and their cousin Hilma a loan of a horse to take them. The horse had been conscripted for two wars and had survived and was so biddable that the children could turn him around when they got to school and tell him to go back home. And the horse went straight back on his own. Unless it heard an aeroplane above. Then it would run in under a pine tree, cart and all, and tremble violently. Luckily there were few aeroplanes about.

In the winter the boys got on their skis. In those days the weather was never too cold, the snow was never too deep nor a storm too fierce to go to school. Mother filled bottles of milk and put them in their rucksacks. Grandmother told them to call in to farmhouses on the way and warm themselves up a little if they felt frostbite setting in.

'The old woman is getting soft,' Father laughed (sarcastically). 'She did not worry about *me* on my way to school. And the weather was worse then!'

So Tapio and Tuomas set off on their skis. If there was a hard frost and a good crust on top of the snow they were in school in no time. They would arrive ruddy cheeked and ready for their lessons in humiliation and multiplication and the names of Jacob's twelve sons and so forth.

But the weather could change and on the way home a storm could be blowing and they struggled against the wind and the snow was all wrong and the skis would not glide well. Then they had to stop at a farmhouse halfway and the farmer's wife would say 'poor mites' and rub their hands with snow to prevent frostbite. This would make their hands swell up even worse and the pain made them cry. And the storm was so hard that it blew them backwards on their skis. And then Tapio broke the point of his ski. So they had to walk carrying their skis through the snow that was up to their waists, and knowing that the broken point would not please Father who would laugh bitterly and say, 'Again! How many points have you broken this winter, damn it!'

But what did they know about hardship? Everything had been worse when Father was a boy. His father, who was our dead grandfather, day of death carefully noted, had been a strict parent. When it was -30°C Father would tell Tapio and Tuomas, 'It could be minus forty in my day and still there was no escape from school. I am not rearing soft boys!'

No, Father had never had it soft. He joined the Civil Guard as soon as he was out of short trousers. All the lads in the parish joined, those lads who came from people with land or privilege, no matter how little. The others were not welcome. Why train people in the use of arms if they had nothing to defend?

With a bit of luck Father could have been in the Winter War in 1939. It was a short and glorious war and the officers died all the time and a smart lad from the Civil Guard could have been promoted in that war, Father said. He could have come home in glory with stripes on his shoulders. Instead he had to wait for the next war, the Continuation War. He signed on for that one before he was called up, he couldn't wait. But it was not as glorious as he had been led to believe. And it dragged on and on for four years. And the officers did not fall at the rate he had hoped for, so he was never promoted. And the defeat was even worse than in the previous war. All he came home with was a handful of medals, same as everyone. And a few bits of shrapnel in his legs.

Somehow he blamed Grandmother for this. He had not been let go to join the war when the time was right for him. Because he was too young then. Because he did not have the right birthday and whose fault was that?

Father shot a black look at Grandmother.

4

Grandmother was an angry woman. She was angry with Father most days. When he wanted to buy tools she said new tools is it now? What next? And where would the money for that come from.

And he could forget about her signing over the farm to him. Over her dead body would he get the farm. As long as she was walking and breathing the farm was hers.

But most of all she was angry with grandfather because he was dead. She had been angry with him while he was alive too. So many reasons. Where to begin? All grandfather could do was smoke and talk. And what use is that if you don't have a big farm to back up your opinions.

Grandfather had been one of many younger sons from a big farm. When he got his inheritance he went to Saint Petersburg and bought a gold fob watch for himself and a Swiss wristwatch for Grandmother. Grandmother was a pretty girl from a big farm and a good catch. She was mesmerised by the watch and grandfather was a dapper little man who had been to Agricultural College.

So they got married, worse luck, and Grandmother was the sorry woman and the babies kept coming. Father was the firstborn. A son! But Grandmother did not like the look of him. When his dark slate grey eyes turned a pale shade of grey she liked him less.

After a few years living with Grandmother on his folk's land, Grandfather was given his own farm. It was a smallholding that had been rented out to a hardworking crofter who had cleared the land and dug ditches and made fields. He had built a sauna and a barn and a shed by the lake for keeping his fishing gear in. His little cottage had been pulled down to build a proper house for the young couple.

Everything else around our farm bore his axe marks in the timbers. When we sat in the sauna we saw the faint outline of the crofter's initials above the tiny window.

'Was he angry about leaving?' I asked Grandmother.

There was a long silence. Then Grandmother said that who could tell but he was probably a communist anyway.

So Grandfather and Grandmother had come to live on the

crofter's land. After a few years they were given three more fields that Grandfather said he would measure the way he had been taught in Agricultural College. With much huffing and puffing and with paper and pen and strings and poles he set to.

Grandmother said he should harness the horse and plough a field instead and get the potatoes into the ground. But no. Grandfather said that yes he had noticed that they had five children to feed but he was no mere brute or farm hand. He had a bit of knowledge between his ears and he was going to use it. So even though the weather was rotten and the rain started coming down heavy he went out to walk his new land.

And so it came about that his Agricultural College training killed him. He got drenched to the skin and he was cursing. And then he had to do it again because he arrived at an impossible figure the first time. Poor Grandfather.

Did Grandmother heat the sauna while he was out? Did she have dry clothes ready for him and hot coffee? And a warm bed?

I don't think so, because he came down with pneumonia and died. Just like that, a chill, a little cough, a temperature and he was gone. He made death look so easy and effortless and that is the true artistry, of course. To make it look easy.

But he was only 38, and he left Grandmother a widow with five children on an Iron Age farm.

The bastard.

5

Father said we must obey instantly. Not try and figure things out for ourselves. He had seen for himself how dangerous that could be. When he was a teenager in the trenches the fat boy next to Father stuck his head up over the trench and got a Russian bullet through the skull. Even though the officer had ordered 'Down'.

Another lad refused to run out of the trench when the order came to attack. He was shot by a Finnish bullet later, after a short court martial. That's how lethal not obeying orders was.

We did not believe him so we were always in trouble. The bundle of birch was over the door to remind us to obey but we forgot.

Tapio and Tuomas, my older brothers, were hardened smokers at six and seven, although Father had forbidden them to smoke and beat them with the birch every time he smelled smoke on their breath. They smoked butts of cigarettes that they found on the way home from school.

The butts made them nauseous and dizzy. And the birch hurt their backs and Father's rage frightened the wits out of them.

Still they smoked. It was their destiny to become men and all men smoked. Like Spartan boys they took punishment as their fate.

I wanted very much to be good but my craving for butter was stronger. Stronger than my fear of Father in a roaring rage: 'The girl has her blasted fingers in the butter dish again!'

It was my fingers that did it. I could not really help it. Somehow my fingers always ended up in the butter dish. I could only look on as those pudgy fingers got coated in that tasty yellow butter.

I got smarter over time. I started asking Mother for a slice of bread and butter when the craving came over me. Usually she gave it to me. I would run out and lick the butter of the bread. The slice of bread I would hide under a bush.

This was very bad. It showed disrespect for our daily bread that came straight from our Father in heaven. And I had thrown it on the ground in under a bush! It could hardly get worse than that. Even giving it to the pig would have been better. I felt very afraid and waited for something to happen.

Nothing happened so I went in and asked mother for another slice.

But my underhand ways and slyness did not always help. There were also the punishable accidents over which I had no control. Things slipped through my buttery fingers and broke. I fell over and cried. I talked when I should have been quiet. I stood in the way of grown-ups when they carried heavy things. And so on. I did everything that a good child should not do.

It must have been a Sunday when the worst happened. I think so because there was a white tablecloth out on the big table in the main room. Father was writing something. His pen was rasping over the white paper. The inkwell was at his elbow. I loved to draw, especially houses with the gable end and front with all the windows and the front door and chimney. I could have drawn them in my sleep, I was that good. I pushed my head in under Father's arm to take a closer look at what he was doing.

First there was the enormous whiteness of the tablecloth. Then the splash of the inkwell and then the puddle of ink spreading fast over that whiteness. One minute white, then inky black and spreading. White, then black.

Father exploded like a hand grenade hitting a rock. He grabbed me by the arm and threw me across the room. When I landed his practiced arm was swinging the birch over me like a windmill in a storm. The curses came in a stream of staccato Finnish, 'voi saatanan peRRR-ke-LEH!!!'

Mother's face was white at the other side of the room, her mouth like a thin line cut with a sharp knife.

Then it was over. I was winded from roaring. Father picked me up and asked was I Daddy's girl. I had the gulps now and I could not speak. Father said answer me but my mind was blank, my arms hung dead by my sides. I was black inside from the hatred. Father hugged me anyway and cooed, 'You are a good little girl.'

He was in a good mood.

Mother put me to bed then.

'It's the war,' she said, 'Father's nerves are shot.' It was from all the bad things he had seen and been through. In Karelia the Russians had speared little children like me. Could I imagine that? Speared through their backsides up through their mouths and left to dry in the cold air. Could I not see that we were better off with Father rather than the Russians?

It took me a long time to go asleep. I listened to the rustling of the insects we called 'russakka' in the moss between the timbers and the creaking of the house that sounded like groans.

Mother had given me something to think about.

6

The sun never set on our arctic idyll in the summer. The 'nightless nights' were bright and relentless. Those who were able for it worked all the hours God gave them to bring in the hay and the barley from the fields. I spent many hours on my own in the house, talking to myself and my doll, lying on the floor whispering stories into the dark cracks between floorboards. The buzzing of the flies and their soft hairy feet crawling across my face made me sleepy...

I woke when a shadow fell over me. I knew straight away something strange was about because of the smell. I looked up at the creature in black standing over me. She was as wide as she was tall. Her skirts went down all the way to the floor. She wore a black coat although it was the middle of summer. She seemed to wear any amount of layers of clothes. She was scary! The smell was the worst. Rank, musty, mouldy, fishy.

I ran in behind the baking oven and peered out at her.

The creature parked herself on the bench by the door. She kept muttering and drooling. She was not leaving until she got coffee, she hissed. She was here for the day so. Her bare feet were green because she walked in the grass beside the road to save on shoe leather like all witches. She carried her boots on a string around her neck.

The dust sparkled around her in the sunlight. Or was it… electricity?

I stayed behind the baking oven and covered my eyes. She had been to our house before. Father said she was a witch—a 'noita-akka'. He had once seen with his own eyes how she had rid a house of spooky noises. She had caught the noises in a leather purse and carried it down to the lake. She had said the magic words that would drown the noises and when the purse was thrown on the water it had sizzled and shot across before it sank. There were no noises in that house after that.

This was backwardness and superstition, Father said. He did not believe in this nonsense. He said best not to have anything to do with the witch.

I closed my eyes for a long time hoping she would go away. Every time I stuck my head out from behind the baking oven I covered my face with my hands and peered out between my fingers. She was still there but she looked angrier every time I looked.

After what felt like a whole day she stood up and stamped her feet and muttered something incomprehensible and left, slamming the door.

When Grandmother came back from the field to start the midday meal for the harvesters I told her. She sat down heavily. This is bad news, she said wiping her hands on her apron, bad news indeed.

7

And bad was indeed to follow. The next morning mother came running in out of breath and upset. She said that our two cows had been hurt in the far field. She had gone to milk them and found they had broken the fence. They were in the next field that belonged to the neighbours. Each had a piece of skin ripped off from their flanks. A piece of skin the size of her palm.

Father choked on his coffee. He jumped to his feet with a curse and made across the room to take his rifle down. He ran towards the door roaring. Then he hesitated and put the rifle down by the door in the porch. He told Tuomas and Tapio not to go next or near it or he would give them such a hiding that they would not remember their first, middle or last names.

He ran out and mother ran after him.

Grandmother sat down and we stood around her and asked her what now.

Tuomas and Tapio kept looking over at the rifle. We waited. Father came back and had a row with Grandmother. If he had the right tools that fence would have been mended long ago. Grandmother said that a useless man blames his tools.

We went behind the baking stove to hide and covered our ears.

Mother came back after milking and put the coffee on.

Father said that if the witch came back to try and nail those pieces of skin to the barn door or to do some other trickery she would get a bullet in the arse.

'But she is just a poor unfortunate old woman,' mother said. Father told her to stop talking because she knew nothing.

Father was always telling Mother to shut up. He had married her for her good looks and plucky attitude. Then he set to, trying his damndest to destroy both the looks and the attitude.

When Father was thirteen his own father had died and Father became the man of the house. But his mother, our grandmother, was still his boss.

When Mother was thirteen she was the second eldest girl in a family of seven children. Her father was a shoemaker, and worked away from home for weeks on end. He travelled to farms where a bundle of hides would be waiting and he would set to, making shoes and boots for the farmer's household. All sizes, all made to measure. He was good at his craft and when there was work he was paid well enough to keep his family fed. And he never beat them and they were happy.

Then his wife, our mother's mother, caught the flu and died.

Without a wife, a travelling shoemaker could not keep his children. There had not been time to grieve because money was running out. So the little ones were given away to be fostered by farmers, who would keep them because it was their Christian duty. Also they would get a bit of work out of them in a year or two, for a relatively small investment.

And Mother and her sister Mariatta packed their rucksacks and went out to find work. And work there was plenty of in those days! Lots of work for strapping girls of thirteen and fourteen who could work hard seven days a week for a bowl of food and a few markka a month.

So Mother was alone in the world then. She was the master of her own fate but not in circumstances of her choosing.

Still, she was her own boss.

Father had been as far as Karelia with the army. Mother had only moved around Finland.

Father had travelled far on the guided package tour arranged by the army with the bullets flying around his ears.

Mother had been the solo backpacker, a young girl alone in the world and nobody to tell her what to do. She got a shadow on her lung and was sent to a sanatorium far away. When she was cured she was sixteen and was offered a train ticket to wherever took her fancy.

They had both been brave but Father was not interested in the bravery of women.

'Not that you could call a woman brave anyway,' Father snorted.

A brave woman? It was against nature—like a bearded lady.

8

Women always spoke quietly amongst themselves. If they laughed the men would say they were cackling. Then the women would lower their voices again and fold their hands in their laps and sigh. And tell me to go away and play.

Men used fewer words but they were allowed to laugh out loud—at other men's jokes—if the joke was any good. A poor joke was commented on long after the event. The lack of judgement in telling a poor joke was a black mark against a man. Heads were shaken and there was muttering. And if the teller had laughed at his own joke, then God help the poor fool.

The men told each other stories from the war, stories that they had all heard before many times. They were all about the horror of it and the deaths and they would laugh out loud at a new twist, a new turn of phrase.

Father told the story about standing watch one freezing night after an unusually bloody day. He stood all night on a heap of twisted Russian corpses that had frozen solid.

'It would have been cosier without them,' he said. That last line was a new flourish. The men burst out laughing.

When they couldn't stop Father felt it was safe to join them. 'Ha ha ha!' he laughed. It was not a good sound.

Tuomas and Tapio said tell the story about the man with the guts spilling out. Or the one about the horse going mad. But the mood had changed and the men did not want to talk any more. They just wanted to sit together and think and puff on their cigarettes.

'The state of those Vanyas at the beginning of the war,' somebody said after an endless silence, 'you would only take the cockade off a dead Russian's hat then. You would not touch the rest of their flea-ridden rags. Then they got the good American stuff... best of.'

'When the English declared war on us I knew we were going to hell...'

'At least we were at war with gentlemen!' It was a tired joke and nobody laughed.

'And now even the 'Sakemanni', the Germans, who started the whole bloody thing get American aid,' another man butted in. 'Only the Finns have nothing coming to them, the whole world has forgotten us and we have no future.'

Then one of the men stood up and said that listening to whinging made him tired so he was going home to sleep. There was no future but there was tomorrow. He would come back and help with the hay in the morning.

The men left.

9

Then summer came to an end, as it must. The sun touched the tops of the pine trees. The rays shining into our kitchen were long and bleak. We knew we were in for it. The clock ticked and we sat in the dusk listening to the radio but not too long because of the wear on the battery. Father lit the oil lamp for a bit but the blackness hung around the corners of the room. There was less to do on the farm and Father went north to work in the forest to earn money.

His letters home were long and homesick. The other lumberjacks were rough types from all over and he did not like them much. He wrote that he had stopped smoking to save money. And he did not drink with the other lumberjacks because he did not drink to cheer himself up like some sissy. When he drank, he drank to forget and that was too expensive. He saved every penny, he wrote, and he was wet and cold while we were sitting at home all snug.

'Yes, all snug on the home front,' Grandmother muttered.

He wrote that all the best timber was marked to be sent to the Soviet Union, as part of the war reparation. It was loaded on trains to go east to the Vanyas, damn them to hell. There was no future for us, Father wrote.

One of the lumberjacks had a plan to go to Canada. He had a book for learning the language they spoke there and Father had borrowed it and was now learning English. 'Koira' for example was 'dog' in English. It did not seem that hard to learn. Father thought he would have enough English by the end of the month if he learnt a bit every night. Then we should go to America or Canada. Or preferably New Zealand.

Grandmother said many from our parish had gone to America. And many had come back no better off and maybe they were the lucky ones. Because God only knew what had happened to the ones who were never seen or heard of again.

Mother said nothing. Her own grandfather was one of those who had disappeared in America.

'DOG,' I said to cheer her up, 'dog, dog, dog!'

But she would not smile.

10

Father came back for Christmas laden with gifts. He had bought Mother a bag of white shop flour for baking buns. It was a luxury we got as a treat at the rich relatives' funerals or christenings. The wheat grown locally was greyish and poor and the buns baked with it were not as nice. Father also brought a colourful hat with four corners from Lapland to show us what the Lapps wore. We all tried it on and laughed ourselves silly at the thought of anyone wearing something that ridiculous. He had bought candles and bunting of Finnish flags for the Christmas tree. You could get bunting with all the Scandinavian flags but the Finnish flag is good enough for us, Father said.

On Christmas Eve morning Father went out to cut a tree for us. He came home with an enormous tree and Grandmother asked why had he got one that size. Father looked as if he was about to lose his temper and barked at us to stand well back and stay quiet and not to touch anything while he dressed the tree.

Tuomas and Tapio and I stood by the wall and I held my breath as long as I could and then I breathed as quietly as I possibly could through my nose. Then I held my breath again. Then I breathed through my nose again, and so on, until Father seemed a little less likely to explode.

Father put the candles up and the Finnish flags. He was in his element and kept saying isn't this great. We nodded from across the room.

In the meantime Mother was heating the sauna. Without a sauna Christmas would not come because you had to be really clean for a big day.

After the sauna Father made Tapio and Tuomas roll in the snow until they cried to make hard little men out of them.

On the way back to the house they rubbed my face with snow

but they stopped before I cried, so I promised not to tell.

And then we were ready for Santa who would come after dark. We sat red faced and well scrubbed in our good clothes waiting for Santa. The day that used to go in a blink of an eye dragged on and on.

When darkness finally fell (which it did in early afternoon), Father lit five candles in the tree. Any more and the whole thing could go up in flames.

The candles seemed fantastically bright but the corners of the room felt darker than usual. Father said we must be very silent and listen out for Santa's sleigh bells. Tuomas, Tapio and I held our breath. Listening, listening, listening…

But it was Father who heard the sleigh bells first.

'There they are,' he said, 'I better go out and hold the reindeers for Santa. He will be in a rush and will not have time to tie them up.'

After a while we too heard the sleigh bells just outside the house. We heard Santa stomp the snow off his boots in the porch and then he came in. He had a strange broad walk. He barked *Good evening all here*. He had a deep gruff voice. He had a big white beard that was long and matted like an uncut sheep's fleece.

His boots were much like Father's. His coat had the fleece on the outside instead of on the inside like Father's and it was belted in with a rope.

'Are there any good children here?' he said in his scary voice. I was afraid to answer in case I said the wrong thing, in which case he would take down the birch from over the door.

'Are there any good children here!' he said again in a louder voice. He was beginning to sound angry.

'There are,' I whispered. I was afraid to look directly at Santa. I stared at his boots because they were the least strange part of him. He laughed his scary laugh from above.

Then Tuomas and Tapio each got a penknife and I got a pencil. I curtsied and Tuomas and Tapio bowed and clicked their heels. Then we got a bun each with sugar on top. I put it in the pocket of my pinafore.

'No,' Santa said, 'Eat it now, it's a treat.'

Then he went out and we could hear him leaving with the sleigh bells ringing. Father came in and we told him everything, the three of us, Tuomas, Tapio and me, sitting shoulder to shoulder on the bench munching our Christmas buns. We were as happy as the day was long.

There were bowls of rice porridge with cinnamon on the table but I was so overcome that I had to be carried to bed. I fell asleep with the bun between my teeth.

It was the best Christmas ever.

11

The winter continued bitterly cold.

Grandmother was going through my hair with the nit comb. She was giving out about the nits and all the other vermin that the men had brought back in great numbers from the front.

There had been three wars in Grandmother's lifetime. They were The Civil War in 1917, The Winter War in 1939, and the Continuation War from 1940 to 1944. The men always returned much disimproved, in her view. That is, those that did return and their woes with them.

'Was it eight years ago,' she muttered, 'and we still haven't got them beaten back.'

'Would we be better off if the men hadn't come back?' I asked her. Grandmother said I must stop asking stupid questions all the time, I had her worn out with questions. Always these questions.

ARJA KAJERMO

Mother was sitting by the baking oven dangling the baby's bottom over an old newspaper. Every nappy saved was a bonus. The well was frozen and she had to bring snow inside in buckets and melt it on the range. And then the dirty water had to be carried out.

She looked tired and there would be no point asking her either.

I was counting my buttons.

'Pappi, lukkari, talonpoika, kuppari, rikas, rakas, köyhä, varas, keppikerjäläinen.' The rhyme told you whom you would marry—a pastor, a sexton, a farmer, a rich man, a darling man, a poor man, a thief or a beggar with a staff.

'A girl with straight brown hair like a horse will be lucky to marry anything at all,' Grandmother said pulling the comb till it hurt. 'A few fair curls never did a girl any harm.'

'I am marrying the pastor!' I said.

'You will marry a poor farmer,' Grandmother said, 'or if you are a good girl in school and don't ask questions all the time then you could become a kitchen garden advisor. Best job a woman can have next after teacher. Then you will have your own money and you could buy your grandmother a fine new dress.'

I liked the idea. I asked her what colour would she like and she said black, black is a good serviceable colour.

'I will buy you three new black dresses when I am a kitchen garden advisor!' I said looking into her dark brown eyes. Grandmother turned away and said that black was a colour for sorrow. Did I want to bring her nothing but sorrow?

I tried to figure that one out.

The dog was stretched out lifeless on the floor. I asked Mother why was it not moving, had Father killed it, but she turned her face away without answering.

The dog stood up and walked away.

Father had taken Tapio and Tuomas to see an aeroplane that was due to land on our lake. There was a notice and a picture of the plane in the local paper. Father said it must be a real wreck of a plane since it had not been confiscated by the Soviets after the war when everything had to be handed in.

Some men in the village had greased their rifles after the war and hidden them under barns and under blackcurrant bushes. Waiting for the day when the Russians would come back. There was even a machine gun with all the bits and pieces hidden. Ready if the day came...

Three months in prison was what you got for hiding your weapon but that is a short time really if you take the long view, the men said with a snigger. What a joke it was to go to prison for doing the right thing. Defending yourself, for heaven's sake!

But for some reason a Finnish fighter pilot had managed to keep his old plane. It was a mystery how he could have hidden a whole plane. Did he disguise it as a fertiliser spreader?

The pilot was going to land on the ice on our lake and people had marked a good spot where it was safe to land with branches from pine trees.

I wanted to go with them too but it was not for girls.

'A waste of time and money anyway,' Grandmother said.

Grandmother said she had seen three aeroplanes in the sky over our parish at the time when Tapio was born. The peace had already been signed and a Soviet plane had come across the border to help chase the Germans out.

The three planes had been buzzing in the sky right above Grandmother. Two German planes were attacking the Soviet plane. Right over Grandmother's head it happened. I could just see it. Grandmother shaking her fist below on her farm and the planes fighting like crows in the air.

In the end the Germans set fire to the Soviet plane's tail and it headed east towards Karelia in a plume of smoke. The Germans flew north up towards Lapland to wreak havoc there.

When Father came back with the boys they were all keyed up after the experience.

'We saw our farm from the air,' Tuomas said, 'and the smoke coming out of our chimney! And our house looked tiny!'

'The house *is* tiny!' Grandmother said with venom because she was born on a big farm in a big house. But nothing could dampen Tuomas's spirits.

'In the future will we all have aeroplanes?' he asked Father.

'Not likely,' Father said, 'but one day we will have a proper road. And then if somebody gets seriously ill, we could be reached by an ambulance with a doctor, instead of having to take a very sick person by horse to the doctor in the village on the dirt tracks.'

'Why would we do that,' I asked Father, 'it would take so long that the sick person would die anyway.'

'Ha ha ha!' Father laughed. He looked amused so I said it again. The sick person would die anyway it would take so long.

Father told me to shut up or I would get a belt.

Father's good mood had turned sour. He said he was sick of living on a farm that was barely out of the Iron Age.

'The wheel has just about been invented here in this backwater,' he said bitterly, turning to Grandmother. But Grandmother batted back the comment without looking at him.

'We are not buying a cart with bouncy wheels! Aleksis has a cart with rubber tyres and he will take the churn to the creamery. He is passing us anyway and it is no skin off his back to take our churn too.'

Our horse pulled a sled both summer and winter. The roads were bad and the sled went over the cut fields and grass almost as easily as over the frozen snow.We had a cart with big iron-clad wheels but it rattled so much that the milk would have turned to butter before it got to the creamery.

'Even the gypsies have better transport than we!'

There was nothing Grandmother could say to that except 'Ah, the gypsies…'

When the gypsies came by they had well-oiled light chaises painted in bright indecent colours, red even. And their horses were light and frisky with shining eyes. Not like our steady brown workhorse.

Last time they came it was early spring. Father was away and mother came out to give directions. They seemed to be new to the area and unsure of how to get to the next big farm. Mother had to explain twice, even three times. Finally they left. Mother would have liked to have her fortune told but she had nothing to give them.

When Father came back he saw the barn door open and the hay gone. There had not been much left anyway after a long winter. It was the last straw! What was Father to do? He took his rifle down, whipped the horse and took off after the gypsies.

He caught up with them at the rich relatives' farm where the gypsies had been given shelter for the night and the beds had already been made on the floor and the babies were asleep.

But Father told them all to get up and get out and be on their way. Nobody argued because he had mad eyes and a loaded rifle. So the gypsies loaded their chaises and cursed Father long and hard. He would not have a day's luck after this. And away they went.

Father fired a few barrels over their heads and more and worse curses were fired back at Father. Bad luck as long as you live, they roared.

Now Mother seemed to be thinking back on all this. She worried about the curses. 'You should not have taken your rifle with you that time, ' she said out of the blue.

It was because she said that she got the belt instead of me. A hard blow across the face.

Nobody spoke. Everyone stood with their lips pressed together. Just the way Father liked it. Still he turned on his heel with a growl and walked out.

He banged the door after him.

12

Was it because of the curses heaped on Father that nothing would succeed for him?

It was not for lack of trying anyway. Three years before I was born or thought of, he tried to start a new life. After one of the many rows with Grandmother, he made a big move away from the farm with little Tapio and Mother, who was already expecting the next.

He went to work for a slaughterhouse in our nearest town Iisalmi and he rented rooms in Sonkajärvi in the countryside outside town. The work was hard and bloody and gave him nightmares but he was used to that.

The trouble really started when he had to go out and buy up animals from farmers. The rulebook said that half of each animal, meat and hide, had to go to the Soviet Union as part of the war reparations. The temptation to circumvent the rules was great and so were the risks. If an animal could be slaughtered outside the system it brought Father a few extra markka in his pocket from a very satisfied farmer.

And was it not almost his patriotic duty anyway?

But the State Police, the long loyal instrument of the Control Commission, kept sticking their little red noses into the slaughterhouse. 'Let them count heads and horns and hides until the cows come home,' Father said, and folded his bloody arms, 'they will be no wiser.'

Father was close to getting caught many times but he always

slipped out of their grasp. Nothing could be proven against him. And anyway his conscience was as clear and white as the newly fallen snow outside the slaughterhouse.

But keeping one step ahead of the police was taking its toll. Father's nerves were suffering. If he were caught he would be sent to the Sukeva prison, where the regime was Spartan even by Finnish standards. It was a cost effective prison built in the middle of a bog, where a few armed guard and starvation rations could control a great number of men. Not that there would be much chance of running away across a wet treacherous bog that stretched as long as the eye could see.

Mother was worried too because it would mean a long wait for Father and no money. She worried about little Tapio who was getting skinnier every day. She worried about the next baby coming any moment.

The next one was Tuomas. And he arrived, ready or not, the way a baby does with no regard for the circumstances. He was born in the rented room with a midwife present and Father outside in the kitchen. His job was to keep an eye on the cauldron of water that mother had put on the boil. That kind of task got on his nerves, the pointless wait for God knows what.

Then came the shout from the midwife. 'Go get the doctor quick! The child is stuck with the cord around its neck!' Father jumped to his feet and ran.

The doctor was young and nervous. He threw the scissors into the cauldron and fished them out again and scalded his hand.

'More a hindrance than a help,' the midwife muttered and turned her back and got on with it.

Luckily Tuomas was a robust kind of creature. When the midwife and doctor got him disentangled from the cord he puffed out his chest and turned from blue to pink and pissed in the doctor's eye and roared like a bull.

13

Sometime after Tuomas's first roar the little family returned to the farm. Not much was said. Mother was glad to be back and she worked twice as hard for Grandmother. Grandmother never said a good word to mother to her face. But behind her back she said: 'That one is a good girl and a hard worker.'

'It is not her fault that her folks own no land,' she would say and sip her coffee from a saucer contentedly. She now had double rations again because Mother did not care for coffee.

But the deadlock between Grandmother and Father remained the same. The anger festered in the air. That angry air was my first breath. That air was so thick with rage that it hurt. I learnt to hold my breath, to take only small sips of bitter air. I learnt to hold my hands over my ears. I learnt to close my eyes. I learnt to hide behind Grandmother or the huge baking oven. Because both the baking oven and Grandmother stood firm against Father, rant and roar as he might.

In the end it was Grandmother who broke the deadlock. Some way into a row Father told Grandmother what he would do if she did not SHUT UP right there and then. So she took her coat and left. She walked out. And she did not come back.

Father waited. There was a feeling of doom; Father was subdued, not himself. He paced the room talking to himself. He admitted that he had acted 'unwisely'. It was as close as he had ever been to admit that he might have made a mistake. It frightened us more than anything. In the end he went to talk it through with his uncle on the farm on the other side of the lake where Grandmother had gone to stay.

Grandmother would not meet face to face but she had set out her terms. They were stark and they were not negotiable. Father was to leave the farm and this time he was not to come back. Grandmother would get him money to make this possible. Timber would be felled and sold. Cattle and sheep and furniture would be sold at auction. The money would compensate Father for any claim he had on the farm.

Father's younger brother Antti who was away doing his military service would take over when he came back. He had been born with a hernia that left him somewhat disabled, but he would do. Father's three sisters had left to work in Helsinki, Turku and Kuopio as soon as they had made their confirmation. But being girls they could not be considered for taking over the farm. They used to return in the summer months with their disappointments and unhappiness and they were barely able to help with the hay and the household.

'Can you talk to her?' Father pleaded with his uncle. But his uncle shook his head. 'There is no talking to her, she won't listen. Is it true you fired a volley over her head when she left?'

Father denied it. But the rumour was out. Many believed it, only a few did not.

14

And that's how we found ourselves on our way. Mother and the baby and me were put on the train. Father went in the hired lorry from the village with Tuomas and Tapio, two cows and three piglets. Nille, the dog, was left behind on the farm as well as Tapio's pet crow.

Our journey took us towards the coast. Father had got himself a job at a sawmill by the river that floated the timber down from the forests inland. He had rented the downstairs of a house for us with a landlady living upstairs. She had a habit of meeting any tenant's complaints with a sigh and 'I should burn this shack down.' For we were not her only tenants. One of the rooms was let to long distance lorry drivers who came and went.

Our arrival from the interior to this municipality in the west was a culture shock. We were simple country folk, we spoke differently, we twisted our vowels in a way the locals found strange and comic, we travelled with two cows and three piglets. And so on.

Tapio and Tuomas started school and the schoolmaster immediately pointed out the two new boys as figures of fun. They had to get busy with their fists from day one. Tuomas had the sturdy build of a fighter, Tapio had spindly arms but he had the courage to take on anyone in the schoolyard.

But in the schoolroom they could not defend themselves. The schoolmistress asked Toumas about 'Father's occupation'. This had to be entered in to the classroom ledger beside every child's name. Tuomas innocently answered 'Farmer'.

'Farmer is it!? Farmer!? How many acres? And what does your 'farming' father grow? To be a 'farmer' you need land, isn't that so! Correct me if I am wrong! Am I wrong, am I much mistaken? HUH!!! Go stand in the corner, boy!'

Tuomas spent a lot of time standing in the corner with his face to a window that had been painted over to stop children seeing out and getting distracted from their multiplications and Bible stories. Being an inquisitive boy he started scraping at the paint with his nail to make a tiny hole so that he could peer out. Suddenly an almighty box over the ear made him see stars.

'How DARE you!! You are DESTROYING SCHOOL PROPERTY!!!' roared the schoolmistress.

Tuomas was sent to the principal's office clutching his ear, his head ringing from the blow, for a proper punishment. The principal sat under a portrait of the President, Marshall Mannerheim. A few rifles hung as decorations on the wall.

'Now listen up, boy...'

But it was even worse for Father. He had been an independent farmer, but now he had to join the proletariat. It was a journey from one social class to another, a 'class journey,' and there was no welcoming committee at the end of it. His workmates at the mill did not care for the airs he put on. They were the proud men of Ostrobothnia, the cradle of Finnish fascism. They had believed in a Greater Finland that would stretch to Karelia and farther. But they did not like men from other provinces or faraway places and especially not anyone coming from an eastern direction.

And the cows did not like the shed they had to live in and besides, Father had no food for them so they had to be sold and we had to buy our own milk. And one of the piglets died from the cold.

But at last we had electricity. The bare bulb hung from the ceiling, reminding us that our lives had changed utterly.

15

And then it was Christmas again. On a small farm Christmas can be made magic even with small resources. Now that we belonged to the proletariat everything had to be bought with hard cash. Somehow the magic did not appear that year.

But one of the aunts had gone to work in Stockholm in Sweden and a parcel arrived from her for Christmas. Thrill! The boys got a huge lollipop each with a picture of the Crown Prince of Sweden. The little prince looked like a cherub with blond curly hair and he wore a tiny little parade uniform with gold braid. Good enough to eat he was. But the lollipops were kept for a week to be admired before Tuomas and Tapio were allowed to do that.

I got a little comb for combing my brown straight hair. I carefully replaced the comb in its little pocket after each use and put it away in a cupboard.

Then something catastrophic happened. The parents went up to have coffee with the landlady upstairs. I put my well-combed head down and fell asleep fully clothed on the settle bed in the kitchen.

When I woke up I was no longer on the settle bed. I was in a snowdrift just outside. Father had thrown me out the window! The house was burning and Father was at the window inside throwing furniture out.

'Take her to the neighbour's house!' he roared to Tapio and Tuomas.

'She has no boots on,' they said.

'Run! Damn it! Get a move on!' And the boys pulled me up out of the snowdrift and dragged me along, one at each hand.

The fire had got a hold of the house now and we kept looking back. Father was still inside throwing things out the window.

'My comb!' I called out to him.

But I never saw that comb again.

My brothers pushed me in the door of the neighbour's house and shouted that they were going back to the fire. Mother had already arrived with the baby. She looked close to tears and was discussing bedding arrangements with the lady of the house.

I went up to the window and looked out at the burning house. The fire was burning briskly and the flames lit up the snow far and wide. A fire engine had arrived.

Or not quite arrived because the road had not been cleared after the heavy snowfall and the fire engine got stuck in a ditch some five hundred metres away. I could see the firemen standing around the bonfire smoking and warming their hands and flicking butts into the fire, while Tapio and Tuomas were running back and forth throwing snowballs into the flames.

What few belongings that had been rescued were lying around, and Tuomas and Tapio were soon holding their arms out while Father was loading them up with what was saved from the fire.

Tuomas arrived with an armful of clothes and came up and stood beside me at the window and looked out at the fire. He felt that the extraordinary situation demanded strong language and he repeated a few of Father's long curses calling down the devil and his helpers.

'Voi saatanan perkelen helevetin saatanan paska!'

Our host and benefactor looked horrified at such language out of an eight-year-old child in their good honest Christian household. Although exactly what kind of Christians they were I don't know. I noticed later that one of their children, a boy my age, ate raw onions as if they were apples. He peeled them and chewed big chunks out of them until the tears streamed out of his eyes.

But they were good enough Christians to have a family of six under their roof for two weeks while Father was looking for a new home for us.

Father carefully listed the belongings we had lost in the fire: A pair of scissors, two saucepans, a child's woolly jumper, a woman's underclothing, etc.

'It is for the insurance,' he explained.

The insurance company official came and held a long interview. The fact that the landlady had mentioned that she would not mind if the house burned down was noted. And she had invited her tenants upstairs for coffee and then gone downstairs to go to the privy? And the fire had started shortly after in a downstairs room? Was this not so? Father agreed this was true.

16

Our new abode was in an abandoned fever hospital. Was it TB-patients it had housed? Not a desirable residence anyway.

The three small, unfurnished rooms were bitterly cold but there was a range in one room and a tall stove in the other. Soon mother had the fires burning and the rooms became bearable. The small anteroom could not be heated so it could only be used for storing our scorched belongings. Perhaps it had been the nurse's office for seeing the patients.

The main hospital ward, with a separate entrance, was also empty and we spent hours playing in the icy ward and looking at mysterious pieces of equipment and dark brown bottles with remnants of poison in them. There were information leaflets lying around with pictures that clearly showed the advantage of having blonde hair in a fashionable style and rosy cheeks and a happy smiling face instead of lank hair, pale sunken cheeks, ragged clothes and a downcast expression.

Then a family moved in to the ward and we had to play outside.

When summer came our former landlady sued Father for slander but the case was thrown out of court. And the insurance company had mislaid Father's list, voi saatanan helevetin...

Father bought an old motorbike, a BMW, and started riding up and down the country looking for a future for us. Sometimes he brought me along. I sat on the petrol tank holding on to the screw top with both hands and with Father's arms on two sides. We had the wind in our hair and I felt as snug as a bug in a storm. We called in to distant cousins here and there, girls who had left farms and found work in small towns in Ostrobothnia. After each trip Father had to hide the bike carefully in the woodshed because it was not insured.

After many trips Father said there clearly was no future within a motorbike ride of us.

He sold the bike and went to Sweden to see if there was a future there.

17

Now Mother was left with four children and just enough money to feed us. And plenty of orders and instructions. Father would send more money when he found work.

Without Father around we didn't bother obeying Mother. I was now six and suited myself, nobody was to tell me what to do. And Tuomas and Tapio fought back in school all the time and Mother was called in to the teacher to be given out to. She came home and burnt the boys' comic books one by one in the range.

'Teacher says if you keep reading this rubbish you will never learn to read proper books.' The boys said bad words under their breath.

Letters kept coming from Sweden with small sums of money. Father wrote that he was homesick. He could not speak the language so he had nobody to talk to except other Finns. And Father did not want to talk to them as they were mostly bachelors and spent all they earned on drink on Saturday. Father lived on bread and margarine, as he did not know how to cook.

He had tried working at a big estate in Småland owned by a mouldy-nosed old countess but it didn't work out. He had worked in the ironworks in Hagfors but the work was so heavy and dirty that he became ill after a month. It was piecework and the pay was good if you worked hard. He got 800 krona after the month. Don't spend it all at once! He had found another job in a paper mill where all the heavy lifting was done by cranes. The work was fairly easy.

Mother read out bits of the letters to us. She cried all the time now for whatever reason. I began to miss Father because with him around at least we knew why Mother was crying. Hoping that Father would be home soon, I began to teach myself Swedish to impress him on his return. My method was simple; I made up strange words that sounded Swedish to me.

'*Hookus pookus mannerheim aprakatapra svinhufvud ruotsi...*' I could just see how amazed Father would be when he came back.

'Christ! The girl speaks fluent Swedish!' he would say.

18

And he did come back. I woke up one morning and heard voices in the kitchen. Father had come back in the night! Mother was crying because Father had bought her a wristwatch from Sweden. I hid behind the door. Father seemed strange and suave in a way that people were when they had been far away.

The following week Mother packed our things and Father had some things sent over by freight and then we were all set to go on the train to Turku where we would take the boat across to Sweden.

Or not quite all of us.

'Antti may never have a wife or a son so the farm will go to Tapio,' Father said, looking pleased with his calculations. Mother was clenching her hands and her mouth had that cut look.

'But...'

Father glared at her, which meant button up or else. But then he relented and said Tapio would have a say in it. So he asked Tapio whether he was a mouse or a man and then it was decided. He would be sent back to Grandmother just the way he wanted himself, good man.

'I am going with Tapio!' Tuomas cried, because he and Tapio were inseparable.

But father said the matter was closed and he was losing patience with everyone having an opinion now.

We all shut up.

'Anyway, nobody has more than two children in Sweden. Four is a bit of a heap.'

So the next day Father took Tapio by the hand and led him to the railway station and put him on the train going east. Uncle Antti would meet him the other end, even though Tapio could find his own way, big boy that he was. But since he had a heavy bag to carry maybe it was best he was met, Father said magnanimously. He had telephoned the shop in the village and left a message for Antti.

The rest of us went on another train to Turku where we boarded the passenger ship *SS Birger Jarl*. Mother had never seen the sea and was nervous. She was clutching the baby and when the ship left the quay she shouted:

'We are for Sweden now! It is too late to change our minds!'

Father laughed his joyless laugh, 'Ha ha ha!,' as we watched our homeland disappear in the dusk. Tuomas and I went off to explore the ship. Father had told us to find a bench to sleep on because we would not arrive in Stockholm until the following morning.

Mother had a berth in a cabin for herself and the baby.

Tuomas and I were not used to being together on our own. Tapio was his brother-in-arms and I was usually told to get lost or else. So I walked behind Tuomas and he pretended he did not know me. He looked lonely and dejected from behind without Tapio. We walked the ship in silence and looked at the big grey Baltic waves slapping the sides of the ship.

We saw our parents in the bar, looking out of place. Father told us to go away and find somewhere to sleep.

When we found a long wooden bench in a warm spot indoors we rolled up our coats for pillows and settled down for the night.

And so we arrived the next morning in Sweden, a country that had been at peace for well over a hundred years, where nobody knew anyone of their own who had been in a war, where people looked prosperous and healthy, where people seemed at ease with themselves and at peace with the world.

But we brought our war with us. The shrapnel that had gone into Father's legs, in 1944 in the painful retreat when the war was lost, had somehow worked its way into his children. Each one of us carried a shard of that iron in our hearts.

We would never be at peace. Not in Sweden. Not anywhere.

Absence

Colm McDermott

Judges' Comments

In 'Absence' we read about two men and a woman and a dog afflicted with epilepsy—so much could have gone right: friendship, neighbourship, ownership, even love. Yet things go wrong, and in place of trust is mistrust; in place of forgiveness, resentment; and in place of love, loneliness.

Author's Note

When I started writing the story I'd no idea where it was going. All I knew was that I wanted to write about a woman stripped of the things which, in her mind, made her a woman: her children; her husband; her body. As I wrote, images started appearing: a house; a shed; a quarry; a dog; a blue barrel. These were things I'd seen in my own life. My grandmother, for example, kept a pup inside a blue barrel in the back kitchen. Not because there was anything wrong with him, only that he was so small that another, larger dog might frighten him.

In the back of my mind I knew I wanted to keep pushing the characters to reveal themselves, to me as much as to anyone else, to pile on the pressure until something gave. That's how I wrote it, by following the voices and the images until they changed.

In the end, the story became about endurance. A person's need to go on and their ability to go on, despite everything. Since I was on the road so much, and could only cobble together a few hundred words at a time, the story was written in this spirit, a spirit of defiance, a refusal on my part to stop writing until I'd wrung the whole thing out.

—*Colm McDermott*

I

Winter came into the old house one night. It was early November. Frost bloodied the windows and in the room moonlight bloomed through its sores. It bloomed on the three small beds moored to the back wall—four foot by two, and neater and whiter than a ship's sails—blooming likewise on the unbroken horizon of a dado rail, where old photographs had been plotted like stars, and, alongside this, on the kneeling figure of Anna Casey.

Seventeen years. At one time it had seemed so significant. Now Anna knew that years, like air, could be compressed to nothing. She seemed to remember it was a sunny day, the funeral, the air thick with bramblesmell, pollenclouds gluing themselves to faces, dresses, black mourning veils… but this could not be true. The girls: buried in January, wintertime, and the truth, Anna remembered then, the brightness leaking from the dream, was as it always had been, grey and brittle and silent, the smell of earth disturbed, the ground opening and Anna beside it in the torn soil seeing seventeen years later her own figure in a mirror, kneeling…

Even as a young woman she was not beautiful, although what it was, precisely, that she lacked was difficult to say. All the components were in place—the high cheekbones, the robust jaw— yet together they gave the impression of something missing. Instead of gifting her a woman's fullness, youth's exertions had made her hard, had toughened her soft parts and readied them for work. Anna examined her reflection in the speckled mirror. Years of firmness heaped: that is what she was. Her face, her neck, her chest, these pieces of her had leathered. The skin no longer hid the skeleton within. In every sunken feature, a shadow of mortality flowered: a malignance or two.

Anna unbuttoned her blouse, letting the cotton fall slack at the shoulders. She reached back and unclipped her bra. The empty cups toppled forward onto her lap and a pair of large, loose breasts surfaced in the mirror. The unmistakeable crescent of sunblush inscribed on each bulb, two inches below the neck, the perimeter of decency, where a woman made certain things about herself known. Below this, by contrast, the skin was milk-white, pureness itself, and, exposed to the moonlight, glassy. Anna shielded her breasts with her hands and watched her belly emptying and refilling, the suck and pump of her breath. She took pleasure in the notion that her body, the dry root, was flooding with oxygen. Life had not disposed of her yet, it seemed. She squeezed her breasts and felt their tenderness and saw the sick white flesh oozing between the knuckles.

II

Dan Bradley pulled up to the house at six minutes to six the next morning. By then the frost had vanished, turned to mist by the rising sun. Dan was wearing a peaked cap which he drew down to protect his eyes from the glare. He killed the engine and slid the keys onto the dashboard and smoked a cigarette, waiting until the green flashing numerals of the clock reached six, at which point he started the engine and stepped out of the car.

He was a short wedge of a man. A butcher's son, he'd grown up on T-bones and striploins, red meat, blood in his mash. As a boy he had been forever getting into fights. His mother blamed it on all the protein. It made him wild, she said. Standing next to the grey '92 Fiesta he'd bought for a thousand euro, cash, in 2007, listening to the engine turning over for the billionth time, Dan Bradley thought again of how he'd learned that some battles weren't fought with fists but with words, and plenty of them, and how in these he was hopelessly outgunned, floundering in the trenches with all the others whose fury stuck in the teeth.

The mist was being sipped at by the air by the time Dan went round the back of the house. The door was unlocked. He went inside and found Anna sitting by the range, in the blue dress she wore for going to town, her hair tied in a bun. Her eyes were closed and she was perfectly still, as though posing for a photograph. Dan had never seen her as she was at that moment and thought perhaps he'd disturbed her. He was about to turn and go back out the way he'd come when her green eyes flickered open and, saying nothing, she leaned forward and pulled a leather overnight bag from under her chair. One side of it was warm from the range and she hugged this to herself as she stood to leave.

You'll let me take that bag for you, Mrs Casey, said Dan.

I'll be taking my own bag, she said, sharply, slinging the straps over one shoulder. I don't want anyone thinking me helpless.

There's none would think that, Mrs Casey.

Aren't you thinking it yourself, Mr Bradley, in some ways, offering to drive me?

Anna saw the panic in the man's face, small and red and desperate to please.

Don't you mind me, she said, softening. I'm only irritable on account of it being so early.

Dan, recovering his composure, but still wary, said: Ah, there's two of us in it so. Although anyone else in your position'd be more than irritable. It's up the walls they'd be.

The walls has seen me up them enough times, Mr Bradley.

Never did find peace there.

After a while of saying nothing, Dan said: I wonder sometimes how you take it all in your stride. There's merit in that. I've always said as much. As a matter of fact...

Should we be going so? Anna asked, cutting him off. Dan was a nervous talker. He'd fill an hour with noise if let. It's just that we'll have the traffic to deal with if we don't. And there'll be no helping us then.

Ten minutes later they were racing through the countryside, on the back roads, heading for Dublin. Dan had stayed up half the night cleaning the car. The other half he'd spent researching the route. He'd found another road, he said, a shortcut, which meant they could avoid the motorway, something he despised ever since discovering that they were spelling the end of small towns. He'd written the journey plan on an opened-out cigarette box which he'd then hung from the rear-view mirror for safekeeping. Every few minutes, to make sure they hadn't gone off course, he'd sneak a look across at it. Once he caught sight of Anna. She was clutching her appointment card with both hands, her eyes fixed on a point in the distance. It was only when he pulled into a petrol station to ask directions that he realised she'd been shaking.

They arrived a short time after half seven, having abandoned the shortcut forty minutes previous: a wrong turn at Lucan. Already there was a decent slush of people outside. Dan sidled the Fiesta up onto the kerb before the main entrance and got out and helped Anna out. A man wearing a yellow high-vis vest shouted something about him not being able to park there but Dan wasn't listening. To Anna's surprise, he hooked her elbow with his own and led her straight through to the reception where a fat girl behind the desk copied down Anna's details and invited them to take a seat.

You're sure you don't want me to stay, Dan was saying after

they'd been shown to the room where Anna was to be kept.

Anna waved him off. You go home, Mr Bradley. If I need anything there's plenty of people here I can ask.

Dan was silent. There was a hurt look in his eyes, as though knowing that he wasn't needed had put a hole in his pride that he couldn't fill. But there was no helping it, she thought. As soon as a man felt needed he started feeling like he owned you.

After promising to ring first thing the next morning, Dan was gone. It was a relief, at first, having her silence returned to her, for she'd gotten used to it, and sharing it had become tiresome. Now that he was gone Anna could sneak into the chamber of her thoughts to inspect the world, no requirement to be polite or ladylike, no requirement to have it anyone's way but her own. The curtains were hung crooked, that was one thing, and her room was too hot, and the television next door too loud, and everything, the whole ward, even the people, smelled like something gone rotten...

After that the day passed, like things not wanting to pass, in drips. It hardened in the corridors and along the edges of windows, becoming in the one instance a chaos of moveable beds, crusted over with the hurt and the dying and the dead, and, in the other, the impression of a woman sulking over the world. It was all so hectic and so important. Anna felt herself being pushed back, out of the light, she with her afflictions which were not life-threatening enough—which could not be seen except by an X-ray machine, and even then were nothing but sinister blotches of shadow nestled between the luminous spokes of her ribs, pointed at and circled by men with metal styluses who'd recommended the rooting out, the good and the bad and everything in between, the can't-be-too-careful dredging of flesh.

Night fell. City lights were lit; there were no stars. Silence came into the starless place. At ten o'clock, a Filipina nurse checked to see if Anna would like a cup of tea.

Yes. That would be lovely.

The nurse nodded and went out. Anna waited for her for almost an hour before admitting that she wasn't coming back, most likely having given it to someone thirstier, who needed it more.

III

Anna was bedbound for five days after being let out. To save her having to negotiate the stairs, which the doctors said were best avoided, she had Dan pull out the sofa bed in the living room. She had to scold him, first, for taking the linen from the spare room, although for the life of him Dan couldn't see what difference it made.

I don't expect you'd know, Mr Bradley, since you've never had a woman about your place, but in these parts a woman's forever being judged on her hospitality. You go stripping the guest bed and before long there's none coming to fill it.

Anna sank onto the sofa bed weary.

I keep a box, she said, spare, in the attic.

Dan went up into the attic and found the box. It was soaked through with damp, hidden under rolls of unused insulation and copper wire, and written on it the words CHRISTMAS LIGHTS. Dan had never known Anna to decorate at Christmastime. He looked inside. Sure enough there was the linen, cream-coloured, neatly folded, and smutted with rosettes of a fast-growing blue mould. Rather than show them to Anna, Dan went out the back of the house with the box under his arm and drove to town, to the department store, and asked if they'd the same set in stock and if they had could he have them. They had, and Dan took them. On his way home he tossed the originals in a skip.

Back in the house, Anna was growing impatient. She'd have asked him what took him so long only the moment she opened her mouth Dan produced a bunch of flowers from behind his back. She was silent. A dozen tulips, he stood them in a few inches of water on a stool by her new bed, their colourful heads jittering in his hands as he anchored them down. Anna ordered him out of the room then, saying that she needed her sleep. When she was sure he'd gone, she locked the door and inhaled the flowers and buried her face in the linen.

Dan took over cooking duty too, bringing her meals three times a day: a bowl of porridge and an egg in the mornings; lamb casserole in the afternoons; fish for supper. All of it from his own pot and all of it so profoundly flavourless Anna swore he was doing it on purpose, thinking that if the food was plain enough she'd take pity on him and cook his meals for him after she'd mended.

In the afternoons, a nurse by the name of Vicky came to change Anna's dressings. She was a gruff woman, gritty, without patience—she'd kicked a cat through a doorway once after it refused to let go of some foot bandages it was playing with—but she performed her duties with the minimum of fuss. She scraped stink from wounds, disposed of weeping matter, disinfected, dressed, and was on her way, having uttered hardly ten words between the moment she barged through the front door and the moment her Sedan screeched from the driveway fantailing gravel.

To keep busy, Anna used her spare time to catch up on the farm paperwork. Lately, she'd been letting it slide, like many things, but sooner or later she knew the Revenue'd be out after it and they were no crowd for an excuse. One morning, after breakfast, she had Dan stack all her receipts next to the pillow: a fat spike though the belly to hold them together. She was resolute. She read each one in turn, carefully transferring the figures into a hardback ledger. When she was finished, she went over the whole lot with a calculator, checking the accuracy of her additions.

By the time the business with Michael Wintergreen started, a week had passed since Anna's operation. Dan had returned to cooking his meals for one, Vicky was back at the clinic, her firm ministrations dispatched to another invalid, and Anna was left to heal by herself.

Throughout the house, there was a feeling of space recently vacated. Everywhere she went, Anna found proof of life that was not her own. In the kitchen, the spectre of Vicky's perfume haunted her with its clarity. On a windowsill in the spare room three forgotten porridge bowls ranged, their contents turned to jelly and pebbled with the corpses of flies; they'd once been Dan's breakfasts. Anna saw them spooned by him, stirred by him, set aside. Even the noise betrayed a presence: a slow, glottal rhythm had taken up residence in the scullery. Dan had fixed the clock.

It was a baby's cry Anna heard, at first, through the storm. It was ten o'clock. Anna had spent the evening listening to the local radio station, a programme of classic show tunes. Her father used to sing them to her when she was young and couldn't sleep. Anna's voice was not bad, when pushed, which happened rarely enough. At half past seven there'd been an interruption to say there was a storm on its way. Anyone with no business out of doors, it warned, was best advised to stay put.

The wind was first up, howling as it rinsed the long grass lengthways. Thunder, next, trumpeting murder over the scrub. And then there was the cry—clear as day, no mistaking it—of an infant. It stirred in the hollow part, the part of her that longed for something to love. Anna pulled on a pair of rubber boots and a man's overcoat and, ignoring the warnings, went outside.

The storm was violent. Anna's chest was still tender from where the knife had entered. Her house stood on the rise of a hill whose only other tenant was a resourceful heather, teabrown strewn. They stood there, the pair of them, the house and the heather, raddled, and pulsing in the lightning. Behind the house a concrete yard sat, broken in places, defying the rain. Anna stepped away from the house, to cross the yard, and as she did the wind gathered and planted a solid thump to her ribs. She went down easy. She didn't move. She lay there, enjoying the fizz of the rain as it struck chunks of broken yard around her face. She righted herself then, setting firm against the wind and rain and defeated the yard slowly, in increments, like someone just learning how to walk.

The shed was on the far side of the yard, at the bottom of an incline: rainwater collected in its doorway. Anna's father, William, who'd been a postman, built it to protect his bicycle from thieves and rain. To see it then, in the storm, lightning's torch pointing out all the places where it had gone to ruin—the zinc corrugated roof long replaced with rust, the gable-end window with a black plastic laminate—you'd not think that it had been a thing of beauty, once, but it was true, its whitewashed stonewalls and front door painted red as a hen's wattle had been at one time a triumphant sight.

It took Anna the best part of a minute to reach it. The wind hadn't slowed: she was puffing hard. Her sutures were squeezing the skin. Any ripping and she'd be back inside. She stepped through the doorway, over the puddle of lodged floodwater and stood listening to the storm and to the crying that had grown steeper now she'd entered the shed. She sniffed dark: bird excrement and bicycle parts. Something moved at her feet. Hunkering down in the dark, Anna swept her hand out blindly and there felt something pressing against the mud, screwed tight into itself with fear. The warm palp of a tongue flashed between her ringless fingers and Anna felt the living breath, like a miracle.

IV

The next morning Michael Wintergreen was standing in the middle of the kitchen; as was Dan Bradley; as was Anna Casey. Cups of cold tea lay saucered before them and they were staring at the contents of a cardboard shoebox which had been laid on the table. Michael Wintergreen had just finished saying how he could not be expected to feed another mouth, what with the price of fodder so high.

You're a cold man, Mr Wintergreen, Anna said. Putting this on me now.

Her green eyes squared with the window, encountered wintry light.

Michael Wintergreen turned to Dan Bradley for support but Dan's gaze never wavered from the box.

It's not as though I left the door open on him, Michael Wintergreen said. He escaped. No helping them when they go like that.

But it's convenient for you, all the same, Anna said.

Never said it wasn't. But it was either this or the river for him. I've enough on my plate trying to keep the rest fed.

And I suppose the river'll be having him yet?

Don't know, said Michael Wintergreen. That depends on what you plan on doing with him.

Anna cleared her throat; the bunched muscles in her neck corded out in the light. She took a long drink of tea to give her hands something to do.

You know full well, Mr Wintergreen, I'd never send a creature to its death.

In that case, said Michael Wintergreen. You had better think of something else to do with it.

Michael Wintergreen braced himself for what was coming. He

was a colossal man, too big for a room, and was forever stooping under doorways. Even now, in the kitchen, he was standing crooked. His head bulged between a pair of tectonic shoulderblades like a bald mountain and he'd no neck to speak of. Instead, chin had fused to chest, a trunk of muscle and bone. For all his size, though, he knew better than to stand in the way of Anna's wrath.

The dog is not my responsibility, she said.

And what about him makes you think it's mine? he said, sudden light spilling off the furrows of his dome. It was none of mine did the fathering.

It was your bitch he dropped out of.

And your shed he landed in. Look, he said, if I took him home now, he'd only be back in your shed come suppertime.

Could you not tie him up? I hear you've a whole yardful of them up there. What's one more to you?

Michael Wintergreen was shaking then. He'd never really hit on a good way to handle his anger. He was too big. Even as a young lad he could never retaliate, for fear he'd wind up putting someone in a grave. He remembered the way stones flew in above the boilerhouse wall at the back of his house, carefully aimed, showering down like comets, or the way the others, once his friends, having learned that Big Mick Wintergreen would never fight back, sharpened their hazel sticks with Stanley knives and punctured his schoolbag, the way he ran and they tore after him, gibbering like hounds, mad after his big lad's blood... He picked up his cup and, draining its cold contents, slammed it back down in its saucer so hard the saucer cracked.

You think drowning a dog comes easy to me? he said. You're not so special, Mrs Casey, as to be the only one here who doesn't love murdering a thing. We both know you've food enough in this place for a pup. I've got a business to run. I can't waste time chasing no runaway. So if you have me walk out of here with this here dog, let it be on your head what comes of it.

It was at this point Dan Bradley, who until then had said nothing, held up his hand for silence, and in a calm, dreamlike voice, declared that they needn't worry, since the dog was already dead.

V

As it happened, the dog was not dead, but by the time they realised this two hours had passed. A grave had been dug on the hilltop, the size of a wheelbarrow, and the three lingered next to it, anointing it with glances from their sorrowful faces. It was a fine spot, they agreed, overlooking the quarry and all the small rivers that ran through it. They'd settle for it themselves. Dan Bradley was holding the shoebox and Anna and Michael Wintergreen each had a hand laid on its lid as a mark of respect for the creature they'd wanted rid of only two hours before. The clay, which had come from the digging, was heaped next to the hole, and after Dan lowered the shoebox he pressed his foot against the heap and shoved some of the clay in on top of the dead dog. Then Michael Wintergreen did the same. Finally, Anna picked up a small handful of the dirt and sprinkled it in the hole as a blessing. Dan was about to take up the shovel and set to work packing the grave when the soil started to move, the shoe-box lid showed through and popped loose. The dog clawed free out of the hole and bolted away, across the fields, stained with the grave. When they found him, later, inside Anna's shed, he was curled into a ball, in the corner. He'd left long, watery streaks of his business across the floor.

They decided to bring him to the vet, Michael Wintergreen offering to take them in his Nissan, saying that it was in a foul state to begin with:

Isn't a shade of dogscour known that this old jalopy hasn't seen plastered inside her, he boasted.

Dan laughed in spite of himself but one sight of Anna's distasteful look and he reined it in. The journey after that was conducted in silence for the most part, interrupted only twice by Michael Wintergreen to warn them, firstly, that the dog had let off wind and that, secondly, he'd vomited over the edge of the shoebox, *onto my good car seat, the fucker*. This time all three laughed. The dog had character, there was no denying it.

The vet's surgery was a miserable place. Yellow and green lino on the floor, the colours of sickness, cat piss and fear and sweat in the air. The walls were bare: it was a new practice, they'd not had time to paint them. Besides themselves, the waiting room was busy with anxious parents and their children. It was nearly holiday season: time for kennel cough and cat flu vaccines. Nervous children were tightly clutching cats, dogs, rabbits and hamsters.

I don't think that one's gonna make it, Michael Wintergreen whispered in Dan's ear, nodding at a pale-faced boy holding an Alsatian.

Another half hour and they heard the name being called.

Lazarus? An efficient-looking woman in her twenties was busy scanning the room.

All three stood. They'd come up with Lazarus as a short-term solution on being asked the dog's name. Hearing it aloud they knew it was a fit.

I'm afraid, said the young woman, seeing them all stood there, that we only allow owners come inside with the animals. Her pencil skirt was hemmed in above the knees; it shimmied upwards when she moved, revealing her thighs, which were a pale healthy cream. For the farmers, she'd tell university friends whenever gathered for drinks or Sunday afternoon coffees. They appreciate a decent bit of thigh when they see it. Flash of the leg, she'd say, and it's as easy as picking apples. Dan and Michael Wintergreen looked at the skirt, and quickly looked away.

It's policy, the woman said, seeing eyes on the hem. Helps keep the animals calm. The owners too, she added, winking at Anna, as if to signal some sort of camaraderie between them, as women, complicit in their influence over the men. Anna, for her part, was just then examining the young woman's painted fingernails and had chosen to take a dislike to her.

So—which one of you is the owner?

Anna and Michael Wintergreen examined each other in silence. Finally Anna stepped forward, resigning herself to the situation.

I am, she said.

Thank you. Please come through.

Then the young woman was gone, through into the back room, swivelling through the doorway slow, conscious of her strut being watched, and Anna and Lazarus following her. Thirty minutes later all three emerged. The door swung shut behind them. The pale-faced boy saw something through the gap in the door, before it closed, that made him hysterical, and had to be taken outside. Michael Wintergreen thought about saying something witty to Dan about it but figured the time was wrong. Anna went to the counter and handed over a hundred euro in cash and in return was given a box of phenobarbital tablets and a prescription for more.

Outside in the car park, Dan Bradley and Michael Wintergreen were opening the box and spreading its contents out on the hood of the Nissan. Anna was cradling Lazarus, watching the men perform their inspections, from a distance. They eyed the leaflet suspiciously, pawing the blisters and sniffing at the tablets. Anna smiled and lazily scratched Lazarus's head and wondered whether deep down he'd rather he was over there with the others, the men, deciding if this new thing could be trusted, instead of with her, in the background.

Then they were driving back. Lazarus had grown braver since his visit with the vet and was sticking his head out of the shoebox regularly to see what was happening. The windows were rolled down; a crisp breeze lilted through them. Anna was telling them what the vet had said.

Epilepsy, she said. Only seen it once before, she said.

There's no surprise, said Michael Wintergreen, overtaking a lorry on a bend. She's hardly vetting a wet week is my guess.

He looked in the rear-view mirror:

You catch a look at the nails on her, Dan?

Dan had seen the nails, and thought them strange, but kept this to himself. Instead, he said that epilepsy was a new one for him, in a dog at least.

Anna informed him that what they'd seen was known as an absence seizure. Common enough in dogs like this. They'll faint and be out for up to three hours sometimes and they'll wake up then not realising anything has happened.

The two men were silent then, chewing on these details. Anna was loving the power she had over them. She drip-fed the vet's report and eased into her seat, into the pleasure of knowing something they did not.

Soon afterwards the men went away. Anna sat in the chair next to the range and before long was asleep. That afternoon she dreamt she saw the pale-faced boy from the surgery being led away down a long hospital corridor flooded with aquamarine light.

He was holding a leash with nothing on the end of it.

VI

The house was a changed place after that. For one thing, having a dog meant more work. No sooner had Anna the floorboards swept when Lazarus was putting down fresh tracks over them, dragging in yard dust with gleeful abandon. One morning he vandalised a padded bra, her last, which had fallen from the clotheshorse, and when Anna returned from collecting logs she found its scree lit up on the walls. She couldn't find it in herself to be annoyed, though. Whenever she looked at him, instead of meanness, all she saw was a child's innocence, eyes that were little distillations of wonder.

She started to talk to him. First, it was the odd remark, things like, Lazarus, you've me wore out, after the incident with the bra, or, How many times have I warned you, after she'd caught him sneaking Hobnobs from her dinner plate. A sham-anger is all it was, though, her heart wasn't in it. She found it reassuring, her own bark; it settled the house, bringing order to its pockets of disarray. Lazarus learned to recognise her voice. Pretty soon they were conversing freely, she with him, unchecked at length, and he with her, silently understanding her subtle moods and their hidden meanings, and in the evenings, after the day's work was finished, she got in the habit of taking him on her lap, on the chair by the range and telling him stories of her youth. How one Halloween she'd broken into Van Buren's orchard armed with a basket for stealing apples and there had seen a wild pig, his round rump shimmering with sweat, rooting for cores in the long grasses. She was petrified and refused to leave her branch until her father came and fetched her home. Or how, in later autumns, perched at her bedroom window, she'd watch the little tragedy of departing birds, the way their bodies shrivelled to bits of grit scattered across the sky, the way her heart scattered after them to disappear into the clouds. A girlish notion, she said, thinking back. But what she didn't say, even to Lazarus, even then, was how that feeling, the desire to abandon her life, to be in some place that was not her own, still caught her off guard on certain endless afternoons.

The house was livelier now, too. Dan Bradley spent every spare moment in the place, oiling another creaking hinge or tacking new shingles onto a roof that didn't need them. Afterwards, he lingered in the kitchen, aimless, like a dog himself in that sense, waiting to be offered a cup of tea or something to eat. Anna was careful never to feed him too well, for fear he grew too comfortable and forgot to leave. Bread, ham and coleslaw, all of it shop-bought, was what he got. Anna left the room while he was eating it, and what's more, whenever she heard his Fiesta in the driveway she made sure to hide the biscuit barrel in the washing machine, warning Lazarus to say nothing.

That man has the sweetest tooth, she'd say. He'll eat the whole lot if he's let.

Michael Wintergreen's visits, on the other hand, were more structured: he had a routine. He called between the hours of five and six, each day, just as the light was fading: the Nissan's headlights looming bright on the kitchen walls. Even the conversation was fixed. First Michael Wintergreen asked after Anna's welfare, whether she'd enough logs for the evening, or whether she needed him to run into town for anything, and she'd reply, polite, in her own inflexible way, that she was fine but thanking him all the same for his concern. And when, in the silence that followed, and follow it most surely did, and uneasily too, there was general fidgeting, of thumbnail dirt and of fingertips, this was their two prides, his and hers, meeting and sparking against each other, and, finally, since it was Anna's house and there is no beating a woman in her own house, Michael Wintergreen conceded defeat and asked if he could be let see the dog, which, as they both knew, had been his plan from the start.

You've no need to ask my permission, Anna said slyly, one afternoon, after this charade had been conducted for the tenth time. Wasn't he at one stage as much your dog as he was mine?

She walked with him out to the shed, to the blue barrel filled with straw, which was Lazarus's bed. They stepped inside, Michael Wintergreen stooping under the lintel. Anna lifted Lazarus out and passed him to Michael Wintergreen who with one arm held him out through the door and examined him in the yardlight.

Make a fine dog when he's grown, he said.

Lazarus's legs were kneading the air in slow churning strokes.

He's a fine dog as he is, Anna said. Never an ounce of trouble out of him.

Michael Wintergreen flipped Lazarus upside-down and held him by the hind leg and eyed his upturned haunch. He nodded by way of approval.

No doubting it, he said, setting Lazarus down. Lazarus dodged back into the shadows, behind Anna's legs. He'll make a fine worker so he will.

Anna eyed the dog for a moment before turning to Michael Wintergreen and saying: This is no working dog.

Michael Wintergreen said, All dogs are working dogs. It's their nature. They want to work.

Not this one. This dog's nature is to be a lazy dog. And he's going be let be lazy. He'll get good and fat and sit in with me by the range and laugh at all them other dogs out working for a living.

Michael Wintergreen's face set hard. The evening was cold. His breath smoked up before him and drifted through the door.

You'll be having him back to me, he said. When this winter's out. A dog like this has got to be worked. It'd be a sin not to.

A sin? Anna said. You've got a nerve to be lecturing me on sin, Mr Wintergreen, since if it were up to you you'd have had him drowned. That's a sin, if you ask me. Only I took him in and paid the vet to have him looked at there'd be no dog and no talk of training him or working him. Besides, you don't get to say what's to be done with him since he's not your dog any more.

With all due respect, Mrs Casey, he's as much my dog as he is yours. He's got my bitch's blood in him, making him my property, halfways at least.

With all due respect to you, Mr Wintergreen, said Anna, one half of a bitch's blood makes no difference as to your owning him. He could be full up with the blood of one of your dogs and he still wouldn't be yours. Them that feeds them, them that waters them and houses them and walks them, they're the owners. Them that pays for them and looks after them has got the right to call themselves the owner. And none but them. I've a signed prescription from the vet stating as much. You'd have to buy him off me if you wanted him back, except you couldn't even do that, since I'm not selling him.

As Michael Wintergreen was getting ready to leave Anna knocked on the driver window and had him lower it so she could put her head inside.

I meant what I said, she said. You've no need to ask my permission to see the dog. She paused and leaned closer, whispering. But don't ever come here and try and take him from me again.

Michael Wintergreen exhaled slowly, pursuing the thread of calm that was rapidly slipping from his grasp. His eyes were locked to the windscreen, his bloodless knuckles to the wheel.

You can't tie me in knots, he said. His voice shook for a moment, before steadying. It went on: Not like you do to that poor bastard Dan Bradley. I'm not like him. I won't take it.

He started the engine.

You might think you're tough, he said, up here in your castle. You don't know the first thing about toughness.

He sped away. Michael Wintergreen continued to visit Lazarus, occasionally, but stopped calling in at the house to ask after Anna's welfare. Instead, he parked his Nissan out at the road and, waiting to make sure she was inside, crossed the mucky path, up through the heather, unseen.

VII

The medicine worked; the blackouts became less frequent. Anna recorded the number of days since Lazarus's last episode by drawing a red X over the date on calendar. He'd gone a full week without a flicker when Anna started to adjust his medication.

The problem was that it was too effective. Lazarus spent most evenings asleep beside the range. One afternoon, Anna had Dan take her to the town library. She'd looked up Phenobarbital on the internet and read that it had at one time been used as a tranquilliser and that its side effects, some of them, were as bad as the condition it was meant to treat: depression; nightmares; near-constant drowsiness. Not that Anna had ever known a dog to get depressed or have nightmares—she wasn't sure there were enough thoughts in their heads for one to sour—but that didn't stop her believing it was possible. She'd never known a dog to get epilepsy before and, well, now she knew different. So really anything was possible.

She started by reducing his dose by half a tablet. She was no vet. Her observations were far from being scientific. But she knew Lazarus, and when after the first reduction there was no change she did the same again. This time there was an improvement; Lazarus became more alert. His eyes stepped out from inside the medicine's cloud quicker and took back their lustre. He slept less and there was no return of the blackouts. It was only when Anna reduced the dose a third time that his behaviour changed significantly. He became restless and irritable. Free from his blue barrel he went missing for hours at a stretch, tearing across the fields, into the quarry, and even out onto the busy main road. Alarmed, Anna upped his medicine, and order was restored.

She was working too hard. Where before the operation she'd have been satisfied with having chopped and carried in six baskets of logs in a day, now she couldn't rest until there were at least ten in. It was proof, she thought, that the badness really had been rooted out. She imagined herself stronger, possessing the body of a younger woman, and she challenged it to demonstrate the truth of its strength. Her doctors counselled rest. During a routine check-up, a young GP by the name of Stewart, nervous of missing something, pointed out an area of inflamed tissue below where the right breast had been. He prodded it with the back end of a ballpoint pen and shook his head. If she wasn't careful, he said, he'd have to send her back inside. That put the wind up her, briefly, and Anna scaled back her exertions for a few days, but it was wasn't long before she'd returned to the old ways.

There was still plenty of work to be done before winter set in fully. The chimney needed cleaning, she noted, always a messy job, leaving in its wake a dusting of soot at the mouth of the living-room fireplace. Then there was the matter of the fuel to attend to.

As far as Anna could reckon, and she'd a good mind for these things, the logs would last as far as the end of February, at which point—if the soothsayers were right and March spiked icy as it had done the previous two years—she'd be stuck. There'd be a run on coal, she also reckoned, and the coalman, who'd already lit prayer candles in hope of a cold snap, would be perched happily on his mound of black gold, lording it over them until they met his price. She bought nine bags from him right off—he threw in a tenth for nothing—and bunkered it herself.

Lastly, there was the question of what to do about Lazarus. The shed was in no state to keep him through the winter; he'd be frozen within a week. At the same time she didn't want him sleeping inside the house. Her father had always insisted on sleeping animals and humans separate. So, together with Dan Bradley, she drew up a plan. A new door was put in, red, same as the original, but this one had painted green trim around the handle, which was Anna's touch. The black plastic was pulled out of the window frame and in its place a thick slice of float glass was installed. Dan spread fibreglass up under the slates while Anna took mop and bucket and slopped down the stone walls in preparation for plastering and painting and between them they dug a moat at the doorway to divert rainwater into a nearby drain.

The medicine she'd been given, on account of the inflammation, had upset her stomach greatly. She was out of sorts. After finishing the final, most trying stretch of the moat—big rocks coming thick and fast at them out of the clay—Anna bid Dan Bradley a good evening and went inside. The pain was such that she had trouble breathing. It took her the best part of half an hour to assemble a meagre supper: two slices of buttered bread, a fried egg, and a cup of weak tea sweetened to the hilt. She swallowed another painkiller, one more than she was meant to for that day, and when she felt like it was taking effect, she went up to bed. It was not yet nine o'clock; all the digging had worn her out. Within minutes she was asleep. But it was only half-sleep, fever sleep.

Anna dreamt she was digging a hole that kept refilling every time she set down her spade. She woke frequently, drinking sips of settled water that cooled her mind, but no sooner had she gone back to bed when the dream began anew, only now the hole was filling faster. She couldn't keep up. Clay was burying her toes, her ankles… By four o'clock Anna had abandoned all notions of rest. She lay curled up on the bathroom floor, shivering, her back pressed against the toilet bowl bend. She found it oddly comforting: the cold empty feeling of the porcelain; the cistern's slow and worried trickling. These things brought with them images of rock pools tucked into mountains and glades. Here the air was clear and water sprung clean and cold and brimmed in the pools untouched, their surfaces polished to glass. Anna imagined her mind was a rock pool of its own, deep and black, filled with the tears of unhappy memories, each one flowing and sliding into the other, their waters jostling to a common lot, but on the surface nothing, motionless, not a trace.

VIII

By the time Dan Bradley found her, Anna had locked herself into the bedroom. The bed sheets had been pulled off and strewn about the floor and Anna sat among them, her legs outstretched, drying each eye in turn with their neat, white corners.

It was after one. Dan was on his way into town when it occurred to him he might stop in to see how their moat looked in the daylight. After Anna had gone inside he'd stayed another hour clearing a stone from its path. Part of him therefore wanted to return to the scene of his triumph and stare again into the cavity and feel the warmth that was the pride in his strength. And while I'm at it, he thought, couldn't I stay for a cup of tea? Dan Bradley had little else to do that afternoon.

The moment he pulled into the yard he knew something was wrong: Lazarus hadn't been let out. Usually he'd be scurrying back and forth, picking fights with the tyres and yapping at the exhaust pipe, but not today. Dan went over to the shed to see what was the matter. He thought maybe Anna was off walking him somewhere, down the fields maybe, in which case he'd be as well to come back later, when she could compliment him on his fine work, but when he reached the blue barrel, Lazarus was still inside. His mouth was moving as if to bark but there was no sound. He's barked himself hoarse, Dan realised, and for the first time was concerned. Why hadn't Anna let him out? He scooped the dog up in one hand and laid him down on a sod of moss. The second he looked away Lazarus bolted. All Dan saw of him, when he turned around to go back out of the shed, was a tail slipping between the railings of the yardgate. He thought about going after him but knew it was useless. He'd never catch him. Besides, he'll be back for his dinner if he knows what's good for him. It was then Dan heard a cry coming from the house and raced inside.

I can't help you, he said, if you won't tell me what's wrong.

It was late, Dan reckoned. The sun, which had cooled to a deep red coin as it sank through the lower portions of the sky, was long set. For some time afterwards, a warm glow burned in the west, pencilling the chestnut trees with light. When these faded Dan sat looking at his face's reflection in the dark windowglass; he was tired. Two pieces of shadow collected below his eyes, lapping up whatever brightness his eyes put out. He'd spent the afternoon telling Anna the same thing, over and over, and being met with the same reply: silence.

Never once, in all her years, had she cried before a man. She considered it undignified, and those women for whom it was a regular occupation were weak and ridiculous. What would Vicky have thought? she wondered. That woman born out of the grit. Anna doubted she would have been too impressed. More likely she would have detested it, the commonness of it. She lowered her eyes from Dan's gaze, fixing them on the sight of her hands, wringing and unwringing in frustration.

Why won't he just go and leave me in peace? Can't he see I'm ashamed?

But Dan was not leaving. As stubborn as Anna could be, Dan had something on his side stronger than that: he had dimness. He chose the part of one who didn't know what was expected.

For Christ's sake, Dan, Anna said, at last, as though she'd heard him thinking and was sick of it. Can't you see you're not wanted here? Would you ever just... just get out, and leave me alone.

Some time later there came the noise of a door opening and shutting. When Anna looked up Dan was gone.

IX

The next day the first snows powdered the yard, the field, the heather. Soon it would be snowing hard; the roads would be made to close.

Anna was restless. She flitted between rooms, never still. She saw herself as a sad showtune, hanging its emptiness all about the house, in the guest room, where she took to raking up and re-making the beds as though they'd been slept in, or in the shed, where sometimes she stood to watch the snow falling in the yard.

Of Dan Bradley and of Lazarus there was no trace. Anna imagined she'd seen Dan's Fiesta going past on the road on its way to town, but she might have been mistaken. A thick lip of snow hung from the bonnet and from the roof; difficult to say for certain whose car it was. But it never slowed, passing the gate, and it never sounded its horn in greeting like Dan used to. If it was him, Anna thought, he wanted nothing to do with her.

She'd hurt him. She'd pushed and pushed, thinking there was no limit to his capacity for indifference, only now she'd pushed him away. That man who'd only ever wanted to help—driving her to the hospital the morning of the operation, making her bed, her meals, dropping everything when she'd asked him to work on the shed—she'd shut him out.

She left food out for Lazarus in a plastic bowl in the shed in the hope he'd come back for it. Every morning the bowl was empty. But Lazarus did not return, and by the tracks in the snow Anna knew there was a fox eating it.

Anna put down her pen. She folded the page along an imaginary line one third of the way down, then flipped it over and doubled the unfolded part back on itself. When she'd this done, she slipped the page into her pocket and went out.

It was four mornings since Lazarus had disappeared and Anna was going into town. It was a ten mile walk, both ways, and years since she'd done it. Two hours, that was her record, for a single leg, though it was a younger version of herself that had accomplished that feat, her feet, at that time, better able for the ache, her lungs for the burning rhythm. The sun was out. The fields, shattered by hard frost, glittered like quadrangles of trapped sea, some sloping upwards from the road, to hilltops, and some down, to ditches. One thing they shared, Anna realised. Their emptiness. The animals had all been taken inside, to sheds. Anna thought of Lazarus. How would she ever find him in all that emptiness? Her spirit sank. Now and then a wind whipped down from the tall fields and sucked the air from her lungs, before continuing on, strengthened by her breath, in the direction of town.

After five miles her chest wounds started to ache. She'd stopped taking the tablets since they made her ill, and now she was paying the price. At first it was a vague discomfort, glowing and receding with each laboured breath, tolerable if she kept her mind on the task in front of her, and took only shallow breaths, but it grew worse so that soon there was no relief, breath shallow or breath deep, and Anna had no choice but to stop and rest. She removed her scarf—it was no use to her anyway—and folded it into a pile and sat on it and waited for the ache to subside. She hadn't been sitting ten minutes when a car pulled up alongside her. The window came down. A hand beckoned her inside. Anna dusted off the gravel and snow from her scarf, grateful to be getting out of the cold. She didn't even look to see whose car it was.

Couldn't very well leave you out there freezing to death, came the familiar voice.

Anna spotted the opened-out cigarette box dangling from the rear-view mirror.

Dan dropped her off outside the library, as requested, and told her he'd meet her back there in an hour.

Few last bits I need to pick up, he said, pulling out of the car park.

Anna watched him go. When he was out of view she went inside and took out the sheet of paper. Unfolding it, she handed it to the woman behind the counter.

Can I've fifty of this in blue? she said, noting how her handbones showed up in the cold.

Don't know about blue missus, the woman said. All that snow. People'll hardly see them. Yellow would be a better colour, she said. Warning signs were always yellow. People were more likely to pay attention to yellow.

Anna went off then, armed with fifty yellow sheets in a plastic sleeve. She walked the length of the main street, on one side, sellotaping them to lampposts and shopwindows, then crossed the road and doubled back, doing the same on the far side. When she'd put up all but one Anna stopped and surveyed the scene: dozens of cars idling in canals of grey sleet, bricks of windscreen snow being scooped and escorted by the stiff arms of wipers; festive lights, strung between shopfronts, flickering blue and red. Three yellow sheets had already been torn free and lay dissolving in the snow.

It's the best I can do, she thought.

They were parked in an empty petrol-court. Out-of-service signs hung from the pumps. Anna got out and stood looking over the roof of the car at the graveyard on the far side of the road.

You needn't come if you don't like, she said.

Dan finished the cigarette he was smoking. He got out and stubbed the butt on the roof and leaned his back on the door and joined Anna in staring.

If it's all the same to you, he said, I'll stay here. Keep her running.

Their breath plumed above them, becoming one.

She went in along the gravel footpath. The front gate was locked, Anna had to climb the wall. The footpath, which was worn in the middle to a line of bare, shining clay, followed the rise of a hill. She followed it to a ruined chapel whose loose boulders had been snowed on. Inside there was a clearing littered with crushed Dutch Gold cans and the scars of a fire. Beyond this, along the fall of the hill, still with the path, passing a concrete tub holding water for grave flowers. Inside the tub a scab of ice floated on the dark, motionless water. Fifty metres on and Anna stopped at a grave, a rectangle of snow that had only recently been a rectangle of grass. She knelt down in front of it and was silent for some time. When she finished doing whatever she'd been doing, in the silence, she took the last sheet from her pocket and sellotaped it to the headstone. She got up then, without blessing herself, and went back along the path, up the fall, down the rise, over the wall, and back across the road to the car where Dan had kept the engine running for her so it would be warm.

Driving back, Dan said nothing. He knew she'd been to the Casey plot, to the stone that bore the names of three girls, her girls, taken too soon.

X

Anna Casey found herself sitting in an armchair in Dan's kitchen, by the fire. Dan was sitting next to her—there was two foot between them, an arm's length—and Anna could hear the low tide of his breath as it washed up on his lips, the fire's slim crackle too, bringing to mind all that was close-in and private. The armchairs had been turned firewards, so that they were not quite facing each other. Next to it stood the Christmas tree Dan had bought that afternoon, a real one, proudly giving out its Christmas-tree scent. Realising that he'd forgotten to buy any decorations, they'd spent the afternoon hanging balls of old newspaper between the branches, using an empty stout bottle for a star.

She's looking well, Anna said.

Dan nodded. I've seen worse, he said.

Anna was wearing a pair of his jeans too small for her; her ankles showing. Her own hung defrosting from the mantelpiece, snow-crusted up to the knees. Now and then a lump of slush plopped onto the fireplace, puddled, then disappeared.

She'd never seen inside Dan's house before. She'd imagined a kitchen filled with things for mending, buckets licked with paint, timber shavings, oil-streaked dishcloths. In her mind's eye she saw a hive of unfinished projects. The reality was much different. On one side of the room stood a mahogany sideboard filled with cups, saucers and plates neatly arranged in rows according to their size and pattern. Next to it there was a small window tucked into the wall and on its sill a few old copies of the *Farmer's Journal*, their pages thoroughly leafed through. Anna imagined Dan sitting there, studying the prices of beef and lamb, and every so often turning to look out the window to survey the land that was his own. Anna felt his pride in the land; she knew it too. That's where the life was, she realised, in the fields, not in the kitchen, with its sparse furnishings, its pair of armchairs, its laptrays leaning against the chimneybreast, its slew of drank stout bottles, its gas hob, its sink. Even the set of lime green curtains stitched with corncobs were pale imitations against the real, bright world they hid.

Dan went outside. He wasn't gone more than a minute but when he returned his cheeks were flushed with the cold. His hair and shoulders were covered with large flakes of snow. He slipped back into his armchair and a cloud of unsettled snow fell about the floor. He blew into the ball of his fists and plied his open palms against the fire's warmth.

Down for the night, I reckon, he said.

Anna knew he was right. There was no going out in that weather now. She thought of Lazarus, alone in it.

Dan offered to get them both a drink. He went over and fished about in the sideboard and when he came back was carrying a bottle of Powers and a pair of glass tumblers. He poured into each a measure and set them down on the fireplace.

By that stage the fire had burnt down. With an iron poker, Dan stabbed at the white bank of ash; a hot blast of air escaped. When the heat had thickened sufficiently Dan laid two sods across the ash and some minutes later a yellow flame fluttered from them.

There was a knock at the door. Dan went to see who it was. Anna heard another man's voice but paid no attention. She reached for her glass, swallowed some of the spirit, and set it back down. She was satisfied. The fire was throwing out fresh waves of heat that lapped up against her knees. She watched the tree, one side of it flickering in the firelight, the other side hidden in shadow, all mysterious. A good width in it, she thought. And filled out nicely too. Nice and thick.

The warmth from the fire was lying in a pool on the kitchen floor. Anna dangled her bare feet in it, stirring it, feeling the weight of it as it rippled over to the far wall, rippled back, cooler now, gushing between her toes. Like a heartbeat, the fire, pulsing. She took another drink, longer this time, and a glow sparkled in her gut. A smell reached her, warm and sweet. Is that me? she wondered. She'd washed in Dan's bath. He'd let her. The water was hot and she'd used the new soap, the one smelling of eucalyptus oil. The scent rose from her skin and she thought again of how fine a tree it was. He did a good job picking it out.

A stiff wind interrupted her thoughts. It blew in through the open doorway: snow in it.

Would you ever shut that door, she shouted, throwing her head back in the armchair. The tree'll get frostbit!

The door closed then. The wind died down and there were footsteps on the floorboards. Anna was still facing the fire when she heard Michael Wintergreen's low growl.

Evening, Mrs Casey, he said.

Anna shot up from the chair. She looked him up and down, her green eyes squirrelling for detail. He was wearing the same thing he'd been wearing the last time she'd seen him, only now he was holding a shopping bag.

What are you doing here? she said.

To Dan then: Dan, what is he doing here?

Dan wasn't listening. His face was pale. He was staring into the fire, arms down by his sides. He looked helpless. Michael Wintergreen stepped forward.

I'm awful sorry, Mrs Casey, he said, his blank face shimmering in the orange light.

Anna was trembling. She backed away from him.

I don't know what you're talking about, she said. I don't need your sympathy.

I'm awful sorry Mrs Casey, Michael Wintergreen repeated, but Mrs Casey…

No! Anna shouted. I told you. I don't need your sympathy. And I don't want it. So whatever it is you came here to tell me you can just keep it to yourself because I don't want to know.

Michael Wintergreen reached out the hand that was holding the shopping bag. There were snowflakes stuck to its sides, melting.

No. I don't want it. Get it away from me, Anna said. She looked around, frantically, for somewhere to run. Finally, she turned to Dan.

Dan, she said. Tell him I don't want it.

Dan turned to her slowly, saying nothing. Michael Wintergreen took another step forward. He was right in front of her now. Anna could see sweat stains in his armpits. She was forcing herself not to look at what was in the bag.

Keep away from me, she screamed. Jesus Christ if you don't keep away from me I swear, I'll jump in the fire. I'll burn the lot of us.

This is what you wanted, isn't it? Michael Wintergreen said. I'm just giving you back what's rightfully yours. A damn waste though. I told you as much but would you listen to me? He'd have been better off…

Michael Wintergreen trailed off then. A hand had appeared on his shoulder, and pressure behind the grip.

That's enough now, Michael, Dan said.

Michael Wintergreen was surprised when he saw the look on Dan's face. He'd never seen him like this, with his blood up, burning red, his nostrils flaring wide, sucking in air, bursting for a fight.

I'm just giving her back her property, Dan. It was she started all this really…

The grip tightened on his shoulder.

That's enough now, Michael, Dan repeated, firmer.

Michael Wintergreen shrugged.

Fine, he said. Have it your way. I'm leaving.

He made to leave. Right before he left he stopped, and turned back into the room.

Here, he said. A present for the pair of ye.

He tipped the contents of the shopping bag out onto the kitchen floor. Anna heard a thump, and winced, refusing to look. On his way out, Michael Wintergreen left a sheet of yellow paper on the sideboard.

Anna broke down, falling on her hands and knees, sobbing, burying her face in the seat cushion. Dan sat on the ground next to her, consoling her, and the fire burned down, and he whispered to her, repeating the words over and over:

It's all right now. He's gone. It's over. It's all over.

XI

Anna Casey stood on the hilltop, overlooking the quarry. She was dressed for the weather: leather boots, waterproof trousers, thick, fur-lined wintercoat. Only her face was exposed. Beside her, in the snow, a robin was burrowing a hole. Anna watched its tail disappear down the tunnel. An occasional spoonful of snow squirted out, first white, clean, then brown, flecked with soil, and finally red, the scrub of blood, a worm meeting its end.

Stacks of snow, five feet high, sat banked against the quarry's steep face; the whole place was buried, and silent. Anna felt at peace. Calm had settled in her limbs, as though the snow had placed a cold compress on the earth, and on her, on their old wounds.

Anna turned her attention roadwards. Its grey length glittered in the early sun. Frost had cast its veil over the stones and, along its verges, shadows of the bare chestnut trees diagonally drooped. At the base of the hill, where the road curved out of sight, stood a small black speck: Dan Bradley's house. A thin stream of smoke hung in the clear air above it.

She thought back to the night she and Dan decorated the tree, remembering how, after Michael Wintergreen had left, she had cried until she could cry no further, and she'd turned to Dan, blotchy from the crying, and kissed him, and he her, and how after long exposure to the heat their lips had dried, and her long hair was loose and wet with tears, and her cracked lips were salty with tears, and Dan's mouth, muscular, smelling of whiskey, was on hers. Afterwards they sat watching through the window the ceaseless patter of snow, the beauty of it as it put down coat after coat of fresh blankness over the countryside.

Anna reached into her pocket. She felt the edges of the crumpled yellow sheet.

Come springtime, she thought, I'll dig up the garden. I'll put down three drills of Nantes carrots. I'll hang flower baskets from the windows...

Anna was reminded of what it was to be a woman in the country. What it was to be hard as the land, even harder than it. What it was to keep a brave face, even when the face inside, the true face, was cowardly, and cracked. She thought of all the plans she had for the house and how the work of the land would never be done, and the worrying, too, over the land, how it would never be done either. In the absence of life, she thought, a woman is harder than any man. And as she stood there, her thoughts drifted across the snow-filled quarry, across the field, the snow, over the heather, and back then, in above the crumbling yard, into the shed, dropping softly, sinking, into a blue barrel, into straw, where a little dog was just then asleep.

The Dinosaurs On Other Planets

Danielle McLaughlin

Judges' Comments

In 'The Dinosaurs on Other Planets' a difficult daughter brings a new man with her when she comes home to visit. This story has no big point to make, nothing is overstated, everything feels particular and right. This is a real landscape with real people in it, and the emotions that rise to the surface here are all the more moving for being true.

Author's Note

One night, as I was putting my youngest child to bed, he asked, 'Are there dinosaurs on other planets?' It gripped me immediately: this idea of things we presume to be lost continuing to exist in a different place, albeit a place that is distant and unknown. The idea sloshed around in my head for a while, but I did nothing with it until one afternoon my husband and the children went for a walk in a nearby forest and came home with a skull. Various bits and pieces clustered around these initial images of dinosaurs and skull to form the story. The setting, with its forest and wind turbines, is rural North Cork where I live. The bumble bees on sticks arrived courtesy of a bee sculpture by Sara Baume, a photo of which I saw on her blog. I write longhand a lot, and try to match my notebooks to my stories. 'Dinosaurs' was written in a notebook with Raphael's 'Saint Catherine of Alexandria' on the cover. I saw in Catherine, painted alone and looking towards the sky, something of the character Kate.

—*Danielle McLaughlin*

FROM THE DITCH BEHIND THE HOUSE, Kate could see her husband up at the old forestry hut where mottled scrubland gave way to dense lines of trees. 'Colman!' she called, but he didn't hear. She watched him swing the axe in a clean arc and thought, from this distance, he could be any age. Lately, she'd found herself wondering what he'd been like as a very young man, a man of twenty. She hadn't known him then, he had already turned forty when they met.

It was early April, the fields and ditches coming green again after winter. Grass verges crept outwards, thickening the arteries of narrow lanes. 'There's nothing wrong,' she shouted when she was still some yards off. He was in his shirtsleeves, his coat discarded on the grass beside him. 'Emer rang from London, she's coming home.'

He put down the axe. 'Home for a visit, or home for good?' He had dismantled the front of the hut and one of the side walls. The frame of the old awning lay on the grass, remnants of green canvas still wound around a metal pole. On the floor inside, if floor was the word, she saw empty beer cans, blankets, a ball of blackened tinfoil.

'Just for a few days. A friend from college has an exhibition. I wasn't given much detail, you know Emer.'

'Yes,' he said, and frowned. 'When is she arriving?'

'Tomorrow evening and she's bringing Oisín.'

'Tomorrow? And she's only after ringing now?'

'It'll be good to have them stay. Oisín has started school since we last saw him.' She waited to see if he might mention the room, but he picked up the axe, as if impatient to get back to work.

'What will we do if the Forestry Service come round?' she said.

'They haven't come round this past year. They don't come round when we ring about the drinking or the fires.' He swung the axe at a timber beam supporting what was left of the roof. There was a loud splintering but the beam stood firm, and he drew back the axe, prepared to strike again.

She turned and walked back towards the house. The Dennehys, their nearest neighbours, had earlier that week sown maize, and a crow hung from a pole, strung up by a piece of twine. It lifted in the wind as she walked past, coming to rest again a few feet from the ground, above the height of foxes. When they first moved here, she hadn't understood that the crows were real, shot specially for the purpose, and had asked Mrs Dennehy what cloth she sewed them from, while the Dennehys' two sons, then just young boys, sniggered behind their mother's back.

After supper, she took the duvet cover with the blue teddy bears from the hot press and spread it out on the kitchen table. The cat roused itself from the rug by the stove, and went over to investigate. It bounded in one quick movement onto a chair and watched, its head to one side, as she smoothed out creases. There were matching pillowcases, and a yellow pyjama holder in the shape of a rabbit. Colman was at the other side of the kitchen, making a mug of Bovril. 'What do you think?' she said.

'Lovely.'

'You couldn't possibly see from that distance,' she said.

'It's the same one as before, isn't it?'

'Well, yes,' she said, 'but it's a while since they visited. I'm wondering is it a bit babyish?'

'You're not going to find another between now and tomorrow,' he said, and she felt the flutter in her eyelid start up, the one that usually preceded a headache. She had hoped the sight of the duvet cover might have prompted an offer to move his stuff, or at least an offer to vacate the room so that she could move it. 'It'll be an improvement on that brown eiderdown, anyway,' she said, 'John was still at school when we bought that,' but he just drank back his Bovril and rinsed the mug, setting it upside-down on the draining board. 'Goodnight,' he said, and went upstairs. The cat jumped down from the chair, and padded back across the kitchen to resume its position on the rug.

Next morning, she started with his suits. She waited until he'd gone outside, then carried them from John's old room to their bedroom across the landing. The wardrobe had held everything once, but now when she pushed her coats and dresses along the rail, they resisted, swung back at her, jostling and shouldering, as if they'd been breeding and fattening this past year. For an hour she went back and forth between the rooms with clothes, shoes, books. The winter before last, Colman had brought the lathe—a retirement gift from the staff at the Co-op—in from the shed and had set it up in their son's room. He would turn wood late into the night and often, when she put her head around the door in the morning, she would find him, still in his clothes, asleep on John's old single bed. There began then the gradual migration of his belongings. He appeared to have lost interest in the lathe—he no longer presented her with lamps or bowls—but for the best part of a year, he had not slept in their bedroom at all.

Colman had allowed junk to accumulate— magazines, spent batteries, a cracked mug on the window sill—and she got a sack and went around the room, picking things up. The lathe and woodturning tools—chisels, gouges, knives—were on a desk in the corner, and she packed them away in a box. She put aside Colman's pyjamas, and dressed the bed with fresh linen, the blue teddy bears jolly on the duvet, the rabbit propped on a chair alongside. Standing back to admire it, she noticed Colman in the doorway. He had his hands on his hips and was staring at the sack.

'I haven't thrown anything out,' she said.

'Why can't the child sleep in the other room?' He went over to the sack, dipped a hand in, and took out a battery.

'Emer's room? Because Emer will be sleeping there.'

'Can't he sleep there too?'

She watched him drop the battery back into the sack and root around, a look of expectancy on his face, like a boy playing lucky dip. He brought out the cracked mug, polished it on his trousers, and then, to her exasperation, put it back on the window.

'He's six,' she said, 'He's not a baby anymore. I want things to be special; we see so little of him.' It was true, she thought, it was not a lie. And then, because he was staring at her, she said, 'and I don't want Emer asking about...' She paused, spread her arms wide to encompass the room. 'About this...' For a moment he looked as if he was going to challenge her. It would be like him, she thought, to decide to have this conversation today, today of all days, when he wouldn't have it all year. But he picked up his pyjamas and a pair of shoes she had missed beneath the bed and, saying nothing, headed off across the landing. Later, she found his pyjamas folded neatly on the pillow on his side of the bed, where he always used to keep them.

Colman was on the phone in the hall when the car pulled up in front of the house. Kate hurried out to greet them and was surprised to see a man in the driver's seat. Emer was in the passenger seat, her hair blacker and shorter than Kate remembered. 'Hi Mam,' she said, getting out and kissing her mother. She wore a red tunic, the bosom laced up with ribbon like a folk costume, and black trousers tucked into red boots. She opened the back door of the car and the child jumped out. He was small for six, pale and sandy haired, blinking, though the day was not particularly bright.

'Say hi to your Granny,' Emer said, and she pushed him forward.

Kate felt tears coming, and she hugged the child close and shut her eyes, so as not to confuse him. 'Goodness,' she said, stepping back to get a better look, 'you're getting more and more like your Uncle John.' The boy stared at her blankly with huge grey-green eyes. She ruffled his hair. 'You wouldn't remember him,' she said, 'he lives in Japan now. You were very small when you met him, just a baby.'

The driver's door opened and the man got out. He was slight and sallow-skinned, in a navy sports jacket and round, dark-rimmed glasses. One foot dragged slightly as he came round the side of the car, ploughing a shallow furrow in the gravel. Kate had been harbouring a hope that he was the driver, that any moment Emer would take out her purse and pay him, but he put a hand on her daughter's shoulder and she watched Emer turn her head to nuzzle his fingers. He was not quite twice her daughter's age, but he was close, late forties, she guessed. The cat had accompanied her outside and now it rubbed against her legs, its back arched, its tail working to and fro. Kate waited for her daughter to make the introductions, but Emer had turned her attention to Oisín who was struggling with the zip of his hoodie. 'Pavel,' the man said and, stepping forward, he shook her hand. Then he opened the boot and took out two suitcases.

'I'll give you a hand with those,' Colman said, appearing at the front door. He wrested both cases from Pavel, and carried them into the house, striding half way down the hall before coming to a halt. He put the suitcases down beside the telephone table, and stood with his hands in his pockets. The others stopped too, formed a tentative circle at the bottom of the stairs.

'Oisín,' Emer said, 'say hello to your Grandad. He's going to take you hunting in the forest.'

The boy's eyes widened. 'Bears?' he said.

'No bears,' Colman said, 'but we might get a fox or two.'

Pavel shuffled his feet on the carpet. 'Oh, Daddy,' Emer said, as if she'd just remembered, 'this is Pavel.' Pavel held out a hand and Colman delayed for a second before taking it. 'Pleased to meet you,' he said, and he lifted the cases again. 'I'll show you to your rooms.'

Kate remained in the hall and watched them climb the stairs, Colman in front, his steps long and rangy, the others following behind. Pavel was new, she thought; the child was shy with him, sticking close to his mother, one hand clutching the skirt of her tunic. Colman set a suitcase down outside Emer's bedroom. He pushed open the door, and from the foot of the stairs, Kate watched her daughter and grandson disappear into the garish, cluttered room, its walls hung with canvasses Emer had painted during her Goth phase. Colman carried the other suitcase to John's room. 'And this is your room,' she heard him say to Pavel, as she went into the kitchen to make tea.

'How long is he on the scene?' Colman said, when he came back downstairs.

'Don't look at me like that,' she said, 'I don't know any more than you do.'

He sat at the table, drumming his fingers on the oil-cloth. 'What class of a name is Pavel, anyway?' he said, 'Is it Eastern European or what? Is it Lithuanian? What is it?'

She debated taking out the china, but deciding it was old fashioned, went for the pottery mugs instead. 'I expect we'll hear later,' she said, arranging biscuits on a plate.

'She shouldn't have landed him in on top of us like this, with no warning.'

'No,' she said, 'she shouldn't have.'

She found the plastic beaker she'd bought for their last visit. It was two Christmases ago and the mug was decorated with puffy-chested robins and snowflakes. She polished it with a tea towel and put it on the table. 'Everytime I see Oisín,' she said, 'he reminds me of John. Even when he was a small baby in his pram he looked like John. I must get down the photo album and show Emer.'

Colman wasn't listening. 'Are we supposed to ask about the other fellow at all now?' he said. 'Or are we supposed to say nothing?'

Her eyelid was fluttering so fiercely she had to press her palm flat against her eye in an effort to still it. 'If you mean Oisín's father,' she said, 'don't mention him, unless Emer mentions him first.' She took her hand away from her face and saw her grandson standing in the doorway. 'Oisín!' she said, and she went over, laid a hand on his soft, fine hair. 'Come and have a biscuit.' She offered the plate, and watched him survey the contents, his fingers hovering above the biscuits but not quite touching. He finally selected a chocolate one shaped like a star. He took a small, careful bite and chewed slowly, eyeing her the way he had eyed the biscuits, making an assessment. She smiled. 'Why don't you sit here and tell us all about the airplane.' She pulled out two chairs, one for the child, one for herself, but the boy went around the other side of the table and sat next to Colman.

He had finished the biscuit, and Colman pushed the plate closer to him. 'Have another,' he said. The boy chose again, more quickly this time. 'Tell me,' Colman said, 'where's Pavel from?'

'Chelsea.'

'What does he do?'

The boy shrugged, took another bite of biscuit.

'Colman,' Kate said sharply, 'would you see if there's some lemonade in the fridge?'

He looked at her the way the cat sometimes looked at her when she caught it sleeping on the sofa, a look at once both guilty and defiant, but he got up without saying anything and fetched the lemonade.

They heard footsteps on the stairs, and laughter, and Emer came into the kitchen with Pavel in tow. Opening the fridge, she took out a litre of milk and drank straight from the carton. She wiped her mouth with her hand and put the milk back. Pavel nodded to Kate and Colman—an easy, relaxed nod—but didn't join them at the table. Instead, he went over to a window that looked out on the garden and the scrubland and forest beyond. 'They're like gods, aren't they?' he said, pointing to the three wind turbines rotating slowly on the mountain, 'I feel I should take them a few dead chickens—kill a he-goat or something.'

His voice reminded Kate of a man who used to present a history programme on the BBC, but with the barest hint of something else, something melodic, a slight lengthening of vowels. 'Don't mention the war,' she said. 'Those things have caused no end of trouble.'

'Perhaps not enough goats?' he said.

She smiled and was about to offer him tea, but Emer linked his arm. 'We're going to the pub,' she said, 'just for the one, we won't be long.' She blew Oisín a kiss. 'Be good for your Granny and Grandad,' she said as they went out the door.

The boy sat quietly at the table, working his way through the biscuits. Kate remembered the board game she had found that morning and had left on the chair in the spare room. She thought about fetching it, but Pavel might notice it gone, would know she had been in the room in his absence. Oisín reached for another biscuit. 'We could see if there are cartoons on television?' she said,

'Would you like that?'

Colman glared at her as if she had suggested sending the child down a mine. 'Television will rot his brain,' he said. He leaned in to the boy. 'Tell you what,' he said, 'why don't you and I go hunt those foxes?'

Immediately, the boy was climbing down off his chair, the biscuits and lemonade forgotten. 'What will we do with the foxes when we catch them?' he said.

'We'll worry about that when it happens,' Colman said. He turned to Kate. 'You didn't want to come, did you?'

'No,' she said, 'it's okay, I'd better make a start on dinner.' She walked with them to the back porch, watched them go down the garden and scale the ditch at the end. The boy's hair snagged as he squeezed beneath the barbed wire, and she knew if she went to the ditch now she would find silky white strands left behind, like the locks of wool left by lambs. Dropping into the field on the other side, they made their way across the scrub, through grass and briars and wild saplings, Colman in front, the boy behind, almost running to keep up. The grass was in the first rush of spring growth. Come summer, it would be higher, higher than the boy's head and blonder, as it turned, un-harvested, to hay. They reached the pile of timber that used to be the hut, and Colman stopped, bent to take something from the ground. He held it in the air with one hand, gesticulating with the other, then gave it to the boy. Goodness knows what he was showing the child, she thought, what rubbish they were picking up. Whatever the thing was, she saw the boy discard it in the grass, and then they went onwards, getting smaller and smaller, until they disappeared into the forest. She moved about the kitchen, preparing dinner, watering the geraniums in their pots on the window. She rinsed the plastic tumbler at the sink, and watched the sky change above Dennehys' sheds, the familiar shiftings of light that marked the passing of the day.

*

An hour later her husband and grandson returned, clattering into the kitchen. Oisín's shoes and the ends of his trousers were covered in mud. He was carrying something, cradling it to his chest, and when she went to help him off with his shoes, she saw it was an animal skull. Colman went out to the utility room and rummaged around in presses, knocking over pans and brushes, banging doors. 'What are you looking for?' she said, but he disappeared outside to the yard. The boy remained in the kitchen, stroking the skull as if it were a kitten. It was yellowy-white, long-nosed with a broad forehead, mud deep in the grooves where once there had been teeth.

Colman returned with a plastic bucket and a five gallon drum of bleach. He took the skull from the boy and placed it in the bucket, poured the bleach on top until it reached the rim. The boy looked on in awe. 'Now,' Colman said, 'that'll clean up nicely. Leave it a couple of days and you'll see how white it is.'

'Look,' the boy said, grabbing Kate's hand and dragging her over, 'we found a dinosaur skull.'

'A sheep, more likely,' his grandfather said, 'a sheep that got caught in wire. The dinosaurs were killed by a meteorite millions of years ago.'

Kate peered into the bucket. Little black things, flies or maggots, had already detached themselves from the skull and were floating loose. There was green around the eye sockets, and veins of mud grained deep in the bone.

'What's a meteorite?' the boy said.

The front door opened and they heard Emer and Pavel coming down the hall. 'The child doesn't know what a meteorite is,' Colman said, when they entered the kitchen.

Emer rolled her eyes at her mother. She sniffed, and wrinkled her nose. 'It smells like a hospital in here,' she said.

Pavel dropped to his haunches beside the bucket. 'What's this?' he said.

'It's a dinosaur skull,' Oisín said.

'So it is,' Pavel said.

Kate waited for her husband to contradict him but Colman had settled into an armchair in the corner, holding a newspaper, chest height, in front of him. She looked down at the top of Pavel's head, noticed how his hair had the faintest suggestion of a curl, how a tuft went its own way at the back. The scent of his shampoo was sharp and sweet and spiced, like an orange pomander. She looked away, out to the garden, and saw that the afternoon was fading. 'I'm going to get some herbs,' she said, 'before it's too dark,' and taking a scissors and a basket, she went outside. She cut parsley first, then thyme, brushing away small insects that crept over her hands, scolding the cat when it thrust its head in the basket. Inside the house, someone switched on the lights. From the dusk of the garden, she watched figures move about the kitchen, a series of family tableaux framed by floral-curtained windows: now Colman and Oisín, now Oisín and Emer, sometimes Emer and Pavel. Every so often, she heard a sudden burst of laughter.

Back inside, she found Colman, Oisín and Pavel gathered around a box on the table, an old cardboard Tayto box from beneath the stairs. She put the herbs in a colander by the sink and went over to the table. Overhead, water rattled through the house's antiquated pipes: the sound of Emer running a bath. From the box, Colman took dusty school reports, a metal truck with its front wheels missing, a tin of toy soldiers. 'Aha!' he said, 'I knew we kept it.' He lifted out a long cylinder of paper and tapped it playfully against the top of Oisín's head. 'I'm going to show you what a meteorite looks like,' he said.

She watched as Colman unfurled the paper and laid it flat on the table. It curled back into itself, and he reached for a couple of books from a nearby shelf, positioning them at the top and bottom to hold it in place. It was a poster, four feet long and two feet wide. 'This here,' Colman said, 'is the asteroid belt.' He traced a circular pattern in the middle of the poster and when he took away his hand, his fingertips were grey with dust.

Pavel moved aside to allow Kate a better view. She peered over her husband's shoulder into the vastness of space, a dazzling galaxy of stars and moons and dust. It was dizzying, the sheer scale of it: the unimaginable expanses of space and time, the vast, spinning universe. 'We are there,' she thought, 'if only we could see ourselves, we are there, and so are the Dennehys, so is John in Japan.' The poster had once hung in her son's bedroom. It was wrinkled, torn at the edges, but intact. She looked at the planets, pictured them spinning and turning all those years beneath the stairs, their moons in quiet orbit. She was reminded of a music box from childhood that she happened upon years later in her mother's attic. She had undone the catch, lifted the lid and, miraculously, the little ballerina had begun to turn, the netting of her skirt torn and yellowed, but her arms moving in time to the music nonetheless.

'This is our man,' Colman said, pointing to the top left-hand corner. 'This is the fellow that did for the dinosaurs.' The boy was on tiptoe, gazing in wonder at the poster. He touched a finger to the thing Colman had indicated, a flaming ball of rock trailing dust and comets. 'Did it only hit planet Earth?'

'Yes,' his grandfather said. 'Wasn't that enough?'

'So there could still be dinosaurs on other planets?'

'No,' Colman said, at exactly the same time Pavel said: 'Very likely.'

The boy turned to Pavel. 'Really?'

'I don't see why not,' Pavel said. 'There are millions of other galaxies and billions of other planets. I bet there are lots of other dinosaurs. Maybe lots of other people too.'

'Like aliens?' the boy said.

'Yes, aliens, if you want to call them that,' Pavel said, 'although they might be very like us.'

Colman lifted the books from the ends of the poster, and it rolled back into itself with a slap of dust. He handed it to Oisín, then returned the rest of the things to the box, closed down the cardboard flaps. 'Okay, sonny,' he said, 'let's put this back under the stairs,' and the boy followed him out of the kitchen, the poster tucked under his arm like a musket.

After dinner that evening, Kate refused all offers of help. She sent everyone to the sitting room to play cards while she cleared the table and took the dishes to the sink. Three red lights shone down from the mountain, the night-time lights of the wind turbines, a warning to aircraft. She filled the sink with soapy water and watched the bubbles form psychedelic honeycombs, millions and millions of tiny domes, glittering on the dirty plates.

That night, their first to share a bed in almost a year, Colman undressed in front of her as if she wasn't there. He matter-of-factly removed his shirt and trousers, folded them on a chair, and put on his pyjamas. She found herself appraising his body as she might a stranger's. Here, without the backdrop of forest and mountain, without the axe in his hand, she saw that he was old, saw the way the muscles of his legs had wasted, and the grey of his chest hair, but she was not repulsed by any of these things, she simply noted them. She got her nightdress from under her pillow and began to unbutton her blouse. On the third button, she found she could go no further and went out to the bathroom to undress there. Her figure had not entirely deserted her. Her breasts when she cupped them were shrunken, but she was slim, and her legs, which she'd always been proud of, were still shapely. Thus far, age had not delivered its estrangement of skin from bone: her thighs and stomach were firm, with none of the sagginess, the falling away, that sometimes happened. She had not suffered the collapse that befell other women, rendering them unrecognisable as the girls they had been in their youth, though perhaps that was yet to come, for she was still only fifty-two.

When she returned to the bedroom, Colman was reading a newspaper. She peeled back the duvet on her side and got into bed. He glanced in her direction, but continued to read. It was quiet in the room, only the rattle of the newspaper, a dog barking somewhere on the mountain. She read a few pages of a novel but couldn't concentrate.

'I thought I might take the boy fishing tomorrow,' he said.

She put down her book. 'I don't know if that's a good idea,' she said. 'He's had a busy day today. I was thinking of driving to town, taking him to the cinema.'

'He can go to the cinema in London.'

'We'll see tomorrow,' she said, and took up her book again.

Colman put away the newspaper and switched off the lamp on his side. He settled his head on the pillow, but immediately sat up again, plumping the pillow, turning it over, until he had it to his liking. She switched off the other lamp, lay there in the dark, careful where she placed her legs, her arms, readjusting to the space available to her. A door opened and closed, she heard footsteps on the landing, then another door, opening, closing. After a while she heard small, muffled noises, then a repetitive thudding, a headboard against a wall. The sound would be heard too in Emer's old bedroom, where the boy was now alone. She thought of him waking in the night among those peculiar paintings, dozens of ravens with elongated necks, strange hybrid creatures, half-bird half-human. She imagined specks of paint coming loose, falling in a black ash upon the boy as he slept. Colman was curled away from her, facing the wall. She looked at him as the thudding grew louder. He was utterly quiet, so quiet she could barely discern the sound of his breathing, and she knew immediately he was awake, for throughout their marriage he had always been a noisy sleeper.

As soon as she reached the bottom of the stairs the next morning, she knew she was not the first up. It was as if someone else had cut through this air before her, had broken the invisible membrane that formed during the night. From the utility room, she heard the high, excited babble of the boy. He was in his pyjamas, crouched beside the bucket of bleach, and beside him, in jeans and a shirt, his hair still wet from the shower, was Pavel. Oisín pointed excitedly to something in the bucket. In the pool of an eye socket, something was floating, something small and white and chubby.

Kate bent to take a look. Her arm brushed against Pavel's shoulder, but he did not move away, or shift position, and they remained like that, barely touching, staring into the bucket. A film of tiny, unidentified insects and bits of vegetation lay upon the surface. The thing was a maggot, its ridged belly white and bloated. Oisín looked from Pavel to Kate. 'Can I pick it up?' he said.

'No!' they both said in unison, and Kate laughed. She felt her face redden and she straightened up, took a step back from the bucket. Pavel stood up too, ran a hand through his wet hair. The boy continued to watch the maggot, mesmerised. He was so close that his breath created ripples, his fringe flopping forward over his face almost trailing in the bleach. 'Okay,' Kate said, 'that's enough,' and taking him by the elbow, she lifted him gently to his feet.

'Can I take the skull out?' he said.

Pavel shrugged, and glanced at Kate. He seemed downcast this morning, she thought, quieter in himself. She looked down at the skull, and at the debris that had floated free of it, and something about it, the emptiness, the lifelessness, repulsed her, and suddenly she couldn't bear the idea of the boy's small hands touching it. 'No,' she said, 'it's not ready yet. Maybe tomorrow.'

Emer didn't appear for breakfast and when finally she arrived downstairs, it was clear there had been a row. She made a mug of coffee and, draping one of her father's coats around her shoulders, went outside to drink it. She sat on the metal bench at the edge of the garden, smoking and talking on her phone. Every so often, she'd jump to her feet and pace up and down past the kitchen window, the phone to her ear, talking loudly. When she came back in, she didn't go into the kitchen, but called from the hall: 'Get your coat, Oisín. We're going in the car.'

Oisín and Pavel were at the table, playing with the contents of the Tayto box. The two-wheeled truck had been commandeered for a war effort involving the soldiers and a tower built from jigsaw pieces stacked one on top of the other. 'I thought Oisín was staying with us,' Kate said.

Emer shook her head. 'Nope,' she said, 'he's coming with me. He likes galleries.'

'I'll drive you,' Pavel said quietly, getting up from the table.

'No thank you, I can manage.'

'You're not used to that car,' he said, 'I don't have to meet your friends, I can drop you off, collect you later.'

'I'd rather walk,' Emer said.

'Listen to her,' Colman said, to no one in particular, 'the great walker.' He had a screwdriver and was taking apart a broken toaster, setting the pieces out on the floor beside his armchair. He put down the screwdriver, sighed and stood up. 'We'll go in my car,' he said. He nodded to Oisín, 'Come on, sonny,' and without saying more he left the kitchen. The boy immediately abandoned his game and trotted down the hall after his grandfather. Already he had adopted his walk, a comically exaggerated stride, his hands stuck deep in his pockets. Emer gave her mother a perfunctory kiss and followed them.

After they left, Pavel excused himself, saying he had work to do. 'I'm afraid I'm poor company,' he said. He went upstairs, and Kate busied herself with everyday jobs, feeding the cat, folding laundry, though she didn't vacuum in case she disturbed him. She put on her gardening gloves and took the waste outside for composting. The garden was a mess. Winter had left behind broken branches, pine cones and other storm wreckage: the forest's creeping advance. She remembered how years ago a man had come selling aerial photographs door to door. He had shown her a photo of their house and, next to it, the forest. And she had been astonished to see that, from the air, the forest was a perfect rectangle, as if it had been drawn with a set square, all sharp angles and clean lines.

Noon passed and the day moved into early afternoon. She listened for the sound of him moving about the room overhead but everything was quiet. Eventually, she went upstairs to see if he would like some lunch. She knocked and heard the creak of bed springs, then footsteps crossing the floor. She had thought that perhaps he wanted to be alone, that the work was an excuse, but when he opened the door she saw a laptop on the bed, surrounded by sheets of paper. 'You could have used the dining room table,' she said, 'I didn't think.'

'It's fine,' he said, 'I can work anywhere. I'm finished now anyway.'

She had intended asking if she could bring him up a sandwich, but instead heard herself say, 'I'm going for a walk if you'd like to join me.'

'I'd love to,' he said.

She put on her own boots and found a pair for him in the shed. They didn't take the short cut through the field, but crossed the road at the end of the driveway, and followed an old forestry path that skirted the scrub. Passing the pyre of timber that was once the hut, he said: 'I saw your husband chopping firewood this morning. He's a remarkably fit man for his age.'

'Yes,' she said, 'he was always strong.'

'You must have been very young when you married.'

'I was 23,' she said, 'hardly a child bride, but young by today's reckoning, I suppose.'

They arrived at an opening into the forest. A sign forbidding guns and fires was nailed to a tree, half of the letters missing. He hesitated, and she walked on ahead, down a grassy path littered with pine needles. She slowed to allow him catch up and they walked side by side, their boots sinking into the ground, soft from recent rain. Ducking now and again to avoid branches, they kept to the centre path, looking left and right down long tunnels of trees. They stopped at a sack of household waste—nappies, eggshells, foil cartons, spilling over the forest floor.

'Who would do such a thing?' Pavel said.

'A local, most likely,' she said, 'they come here at night when they know they won't be seen.' Pavel tried to gather the rubbish back into the bag, a hopelessly ineffective gesture, like a surgeon attempting to heap intestines back into a ruptured abdomen. When he stood up, his hands were covered in dirt and pine needles. She took a handkerchief from her coat pocket and handed it to him.

'Does it happen a lot?' he said.

'Only close to the entrance,' she said, 'people are lazy.' He had finished with the handkerchief and seemed unsure what to do with it. 'I don't want it back,' she said, and grinning, he put it in his own pocket.

It was quieter the farther in they went, less birds, the occasional rustle of an unseen animal in the undergrowth. He talked about London and about his work, and she talked about moving from the

city, the years when the children were young, John in Japan. She
noticed his limp becoming more pronounced and slowed her pace.

'Thanks for going to such trouble with the room,' he said.

'It was no trouble.'

'I was touched by it,' he said, 'especially the bear duvet and the
rabbit.'

She glanced at him, and saw that he was teasing. She laughed.

'She didn't tell you I was coming, did she?' he said.

'No, but it doesn't matter.'

'I'm sorry it caused awkwardness,' he said, 'I know your
husband is annoyed.'

'He's annoyed with Emer,' she said, 'not with you. Anyway, it
doesn't matter.'

She sensed he was tiring and when they came to a fallen tree,
she sat on the trunk and he sat beside her. She tilted her head back
and looked up. Here there was no sky, but there was light, and as
it travelled down through the trees, it seemed to absorb hues of
yellow and green. By her feet was a broad-leafed plant, half of it in
shade, the other half covered in a filigree pattern projected through
a shadow box of branches. She saw the undersides of leaves,
illuminated from above, and their tapestries of green and white
veins. A colony of toadstools, brown puff-balls, sprouted from the
grass by her feet. Pavel nudged them with his boot. They released
a cloud of pungent spores and, fascinated, he bent and prodded
them with his finger until they released more. He got out his
phone and took a photograph.

'I've seen Oisín three times in the last four years,' she said.
'Emer will take him back to London tomorrow and I can't bear it.'

He put the phone away and, reaching out, he took her hand.
'I'm sorry,' he said, 'I don't understand why Emer would live
anywhere else when she could live here. But then I guess I don't
understand Emer.'

'I'm a stranger to him,' she said, 'I'm his grandmother and I'm a stranger. He'll grow up not knowing who I am.'

'He already knows who you are. He'll remember.'

'He'll remember that bloody skull in the bucket,' she said bitterly.

Very softly, he began to stroke her palm with his thumb. She pulled her hand away and got up, stood with her back to him. Still facing away, she pointed to a dark corridor of trees that ran perpendicular to the main path. 'That's a short cut,' she said, 'it leads back down to the roadway. I remember it from years ago when the children were small.'

This route was less used by walkers, tangled and overgrown, obstructed here and there by trees that leaned in a slant across the path, not quite fallen, resting against other trees. Ferns grew tall and curling and the moss was inches thick on the tree trunks. In the quiet, she imagined she could hear the spines of leaves snapping as her boots pressed them into the mud. They walked with their hands by their sides, so close that if they hadn't been careful, they might have touched. The path brought them to an exit by the main road, and they walked back to the house in silence, arriving just as Colman's car pulled into the driveway.

They were all back: Colman, Emer, Oisín. Emer's mood had changed. Now she was full of the frenetic energy that often seized her, opening the drawers of the cabinet in the sitting room and spreading the contents all over the carpet, searching for a catalogue from an old college exhibition. Oisín had a new toy truck his grandfather had bought him. It was almost identical to the truck from beneath the stairs, except this one had all its wheels. He sat on the kitchen floor and drove it back and forth over the tiles making revving noises. Colman was subdued. He made a pot of tea, not his usual kind, but the lemon and ginger that Kate liked, and they sat together at the table.

'How did you get on with Captain Kirk?' he said.

'Fine,' she said.

Emer came in from the sitting room, having found what she was looking for. She poured tea from the pot and stood looking out the window as she drank it. Pavel was on the ditch at the end of the garden, taking photographs of the wind turbines. 'Know what they remind me of?' Emer said, 'those bumble bees John used to catch in jars. He'd put one end of a stick through their bellies and the other end in the ground, and we'd watch their wings going like crazy.'

'Emer!' Kate said, 'they were always dead when he did that.'

Emer turned from the window, gave a sharp little laugh. 'I forgot,' she said, 'Saint John, the Chosen One.' She emptied what was left of her tea down the sink. 'Trust me,' she said, 'the bees were alive. Or at least they were when he started.'

Oisín got up from the floor and went over to his mother, the new truck in his hand. 'If I don't take my laser gun, can I take this instead?' he said.

'Yes, yes,' Emer said, 'now go see if you can find my lighter in the sitting room, will you?' She made shooing gestures with her hand.

The child stopped where he was, considering the truck. 'Or maybe I'll take the gun and I won't take my Lego,' he said, 'they probably have loads of Lego in Australia.'

'Australia?' Kate said. She looked across the table at Colman, but he was staring into his cup, swirling dregs of tea around the bottom.

Emer sighed. 'Sorry, Mam,' she said, 'I was going to tell you. It's not for ages anyway, not until summer.'

In bed that night, she began to cry. Colman switched on a lamp and rolled onto his side to face her. 'You know what that girl's like,' he said, 'she's never lasted at anything yet. Australia will be no different.'

'But how do you know?' she said, when she could manage to get the words out, 'maybe they'll stay there forever.'

She buried her face in his shoulder. The smell of him, the feel of him, the way her body slotted around his, was as she remembered. She climbed onto him so that they lay length to length and, opening the buttons of his pyjamas, she rested her head on the wiry hair of his chest. He patted her back awkwardly through her nightdress as she continued to cry. She kissed him, on his mouth, on his neck, and, undoing the remainder of the buttons, she stroked his stomach. He didn't respond but neither did he object, and she slid her hand lower, under the waistband of his pyjama bottoms. He stopped patting her back. Taking her gently by the wrist, he removed her hand and placed it by her side. Then he eased himself out from under her, and turned away towards the wall.

Her nightdress had slid up around her tummy and she tugged it down over her knees. She edged back across the mattress and lay very still, staring at the ceiling. The house was quiet, none of the sounds of the previous night. She could hear Colman fumbling at his clothing, and when she glanced sideways, saw he was doing up his buttons. He switched off the lamp, and after a while, perhaps half an hour, she heard snoring. She knew she should try to sleep too, but couldn't. Tomorrow, they would return to London: Oisín, Emer and Pavel. Oisín would probably want to take the skull with him. She pictured him waking early again, sneaking down to the bucket at first light. Swinging her legs over the side of the bed, she went downstairs in her bare feet.

A lamp on the telephone table, one of Colman's wooden lamps with a red shade, threw a rose-coloured light over the hall. The cat rushed her ankles, mewling and rubbing against her. 'What are you doing up?' she said, stooping to run her hand along its back, 'why aren't you in bed?' The door of the sitting room, where they kept the cat's basket, was partly open. She listened, and thought she heard something stirring. The cat had been winding itself in and out around her legs and now it made a quick foray into the room, came running out again, voicing small noises of complaint. She went to the door and, in the light filtering in from the hall, saw a shape on the sofa. It was Pavel with a rug over him, using one of the cushions as a pillow.

He sat up and reached for his glasses from the coffee table. He appeared confused, as if he had just woken, but she noticed how his expression changed when he realised it was her. She remained in the doorway, conscious, even in the semi-darkness, of his eyes moving over the thin cotton of her nightdress. The house was completely still and the cat had quietened, settling itself on the carpet by her feet. Pavel stared at her but didn't speak. They stayed like that, neither of them moving, and she understood that he was waiting, allowing her to decide. After a moment, she turned and walked down the hall to the kitchen, the cat padding after her.

In the utility room, she put on a pair of rubber gloves and, dipping her hand into the bucket, lifted out the skull. It dripped bleach onto the floor and she got a towel and dried it off, wiping the rims of its eye sockets, the crevices of the jaws. She sat it on top of the washing machine and looked at it, and it returned her gaze with empty, cavernous eyes. Not bothering with a coat, she slipped her feet into Colman's wellingtons and carried the bucket of bleach outside.

It was cold, hinting at late frost, and she shivered in her nightdress. In the field behind the house, the pile of newly-chopped wood appeared almost white in the moonlight, and moonlight glinted on the galvanised roof of Dennehys' shed and silvered the tops of the trees in the forest. She tipped the bucket over, spilling the bleach onto the ground. For a second it lay upon the surface, before gradually seeping away until only a flotsam of dead insects speckled the stones. Putting down the bucket, she gazed up at the night sky. There were stars, millions of them, the familiar constellations she had known since childhood. From this distance, they appeared cold and still and beautiful, but she had read somewhere that they were always moving, held together only by their own gravity. They were white-hot clouds of dust and gas, and the light, if you got close, would blind you.

Notes on the Authors

Sara Baume was born in Lancashire, England, in 1984. She grew up in County Cork and studied Fine Art in IADT Dun Laoghaire before completing the MPhil in Creative Writing at Trinity College. Her short stories have been published in *The Moth, The Penny Dreadful, The Stinging Fly, the Dublin Review* and the *Irish Independent* as part of the Hennessy New Irish Writing series. Her reviews and articles on visual art and books have also appeared online and in print. Her debut novel, *Spill Simmer Falter Wither*, will be published by Tramp Press in 2015.

Trevor Byrne was born in Dublin in 1981. His debut novel, *Ghosts and Lightning*, is published by Canongate, and was selected as a Book of the Year in *The Irish Times* and *The Guardian*. Trevor is co-founder and senior editor at The Editing Firm. He's currently working on his second novel, and a series of short stories.

Julian Gough sang on four albums by Toasted Heretic. He is the author of three novels, *Juno & Juliet, Jude in Ireland*, and *Jude in London*, and a poetry collection, *Free Sex Chocolate*. He has won the BBC National Short Story Award, and been shortlisted, twice, for the Everyman Bollinger Wodehouse Prize. He lives in Berlin.

Arja Kajermo was born in Finland, grew up in Sweden and moved to Ireland in her twenties. She started drawing cartoons for *In Dublin* magazine. A collection of these strips were published as *Dirty Dublin Strip Cartoons*. She contributed cartoons to many other Irish publications. She now draws for Swedish newspaper *Dagens Nyheter* and has three cartoon books published in Sweden.

Colm McDermott was born in 1988 and grew up in Clane, County Kildare. In 2010 he completed a Pharmacy degree in Trinity College Dublin and worked for a time in the pharmaceutical sector. 'Absence' is his first published story. It was written on the road, in cafés and guesthouses, on planes and buses, travelling across Indonesia, Borneo and the Philippines. He has recently returned to live in Dublin.

Danielle McLaughlin's short stories have appeared in various newspapers, journals and anthologies, most recently *The Fog Horn*, *The Penny Dreadful*, *The South Circular*, *Southword*, *The Irish Times* and *The New Yorker*. Her first collection will be published by The Stinging Fly Press in 2015. She lives in Cork with her husband and three children.

Acknowledgements

Thanks once again to Redmond Doran and the Doran family for continuing their very generous sponsorship of the Davy Byrnes Short Story Award. Thanks also to Jane Alger and Elizabeth Cuddy of Dublin UNESCO City of Literature for their cooperation and support in organising the competition. Our panel of readers this year were Lisa Coen, Fiona Dunne, Thomas Morris and Sean O'Reilly.

I was delighted that Anne Enright, Yiyun Li and Jon McGregor agreed to act as our final adjudicators. They have been extremely generous with their time throughout the process.

Thanks to Peter O'Connell for his great work publicising the award and to Fergal Condon for designing the lovely cover of this here book.

Declan Meade
Publisher & Competition Administrator

The Stinging Fly magazine was established in 1997 to seek out, publish and promote the very best new Irish and international writing. We have a particular interest in encouraging new writers, and in promoting the short story form. We publish three issues of *The Stinging Fly* each year: in February, June and October.

The Stinging Fly Press was launched in May 2005 with the publication of our first title, *Watermark* by Sean O'Reilly. In 2007 we published Kevin Barry's debut short story collection, *There Are Little Kingdoms*; and in 2009, *Life in The Universe* by Michael J. Farrell. *The China Factory*, a collection of stories by Mary Costello, was nominated for The Guardian First Book Award in 2012. Our most recent book, *Young Skins* by Colin Barrett, has won the 2014 Frank O'Connor International Short Story Award and the 2014 Rooney Prize for Irish Literature. In addition to these, we have published a number of short story anthologies.

All Stinging Fly Press titles can be purchased online from our website. Our books are distributed to the trade by Irish Book Distribution (IRL/UK) and Dufour Editions (USA). The titles listed here are also available as ebooks via the main platforms.

If you experience any difficulty in finding our books, please e-mail us at stingingfly@gmail.com.

visit www.stingingfly.org